Belling the Tiger(ess)

by

M. Culler

Belling the Tiger(ess)

Cover Art by *The Wild Rose Press, Inc.*

The Wild Rose Press, Inc.
PO Box 708
Adams Basin, NY 14410-0708
Visit us at www.thewildrosepress.com

Publishing History
First Edition, 2023
Trade Paperback ISBN 978-1-5092-4932-9
Digital ISBN 978-1-5092-4933-6

Published in the United States of America

"Mr. Warwick. There you are." A yellow patch of light spilled onto the walkway as the lady of the house opened the door.

"A pleasure to see you, Miss Mumford." Augustus trotted up the steps and squeezed her hand for a moment longer than he needed, unable to keep the smile off his face. "I've just seen Tiger. Or…whatever you call that one." He winked.

She gaped at him. "Wh-what do you mean?"

Augustus, emboldened by admiration and the prospect of earning her trust by keeping her secret, pulled her from the house and gently let the front door fall shut behind her. "I know, Miss Mumford. I know your secret."

She said nothing, her skin losing its creamy tone and fading to sickly gray, the pallor emphasized by her black dress. With a stagger, she clutched the doorframe, bosom heaving.

"Oh! Oh, please, don't worry. I only just figured it out, and I won't tell a soul. I think it's brilliant!" He squeezed her hands, both of them in both of his. A current of electricity ran up his arms and down his spine.

Praise for M. Culler

"M. Culler has done it again with this beautifully woven tale. The blending of sweet and funny is achieved to a deeply satisfying effect and will hold you spellbound from the first page to the last."

~ Best Selling Author, T Wells Brown

"A magical, old-fashioned romance where opposites attract and love blossoms. I loved this story and couldn't put it down."

~ Award Winning Author, D.A. Nelson

"Delightfully enchanting, witty, and charming."

~ LoLo Paige, Award Winning Author of the Blazing Hearts Wildfire Series

Dedication

To my writer brothers and sisters. The list keeps growing, and all of you are so dear to me. Thank you to Judy, Rachelle, Dawn, Terry, Lolo, Michelle, Sofia, Harry, Steven, and David.
To the man who loves me no matter what, who I will always love no matter what, Phillip.
To my biggest little blessings, Malcolm and Morgana.
To Gladys Felice. Every book is for you.
To my parents, who always find ways to support me. I couldn't ask for better.
Soli Deo Gloria.

Chapter One

Spring, 1910

Rowena dressed simply. Lived simply. Despite possessing a considerable amount of wealth and a lovely home of her own, she never flaunted her well-to-do status. She was quite content to be a spinster and to let the neighborhood children whisper behind their hands that she was a witch.

They were right, in a way. Weren't they?

She must be a witch, or at least have close-enough associations to have been cursed by one. How else would she be afflicted with this horrid secret—a secret that would have surely seen her burned at the stake just a few centuries ago.

Not the affliction of being clever. More and more, women wanted to study or work (provided they weren't married, naturally). It might not be considered entirely *proper*, but at least it was somewhat accepted.

"Good evening, Miss Mumford."

"Good evening." Rowena nodded to Mr. Chesterton as he stepped off the trolley.

It was time for the nightly parade. There were no cymbals, no carriages, no bunting-covered Oldsmobiles. There were just men.

Thin ones, tall ones, rotund ones, short ones, graying widowers, and young dandies flushed with pride over their first jobs as shopkeepers or law clerks. Despite the wide array of men passing the Mumford house, they all had something in common. They were all thinking of matrimony.

She had heard it whispered that *any* decent eligible man in Cedar Point, Massachusetts, thought of matrimony when he saw Rowena Mumford watering her geraniums at twilight.

Rowena had uniquely good hearing, a trait passed down on her mother's side. Her ears had caught many comments, whether whispers behind her back or admonitions directly to her face.

Why, in the last week alone, she could count at least three different urgings to the noble estate of matrimony—and none of them were from suitors.

"Not Christian that a woman so lovely should fail to do her duty of becoming someone's wife," hinted Mrs. Chambers, the minister's wife.

"Darling, you're not getting any younger. You're nearly twenty-seven." That was Cousin Isadore, who already had four strapping children under the age of six.

"Do you want to die alone?" screeched Granny Nesbitt, who had an endless stream of devoted grandchildren and grandnieces and grandnephews dancing attendance upon her.

Rowena stopped musing as some of the "parade" did more than simply smile and doff their chapeaus from the neat redbrick sidewalks.

Mr. Ruger, a very nice man with a thick German accent and even thicker mustaches, presented her with a crock of pickles. "I heard you were fond of pickles, Fraulein Mumford. My mother made these. She has her own recipe, and the larder is full of them."

Professor Trilby rushed to give her his article that was to be published in the *Cedar Point Gazette.* ("You are a woman who reads. I have no objection to a wife who reads. In fact, I'd encourage it.")

Matthew Raine was the last caller of the evening. He swaggered up to her in breeches too tight and a smile too wide, smelling of clove and hair pomade. He swept to her porch railing with a bouquet of drooping lilacs. ("They smell heavenly, but not as heavenly as your roast beef or your potted plants, Miss Mumford. How is it that such a capable woman hasn't accepted a suitor yet?")

At six on the nose, Rowena shut and locked her front door and let out a tiny scream. She had been courted with pickles, papers, and flowers.

"Not one of those men would love the real me, warts, whiskers, and all," Rowena moaned, looking at the portrait of her late parents. Their smiling likeness, done in oils, hung over the fireplace, which was cold and dark.

Rowena preferred the kitchen. She wrote her essays there, publishing them under the name of Robert Mumford, Esq., correspondent for the *Cincinnati Speculator*. Between teaching piano, French, and writing, she kept the towering old family home in good repair.

"It's frustrating to know that they see me as such a simple creature, Tiger." She stroked her beautiful black cat (who admittedly didn't help the witch rumors). "They see me as a beauty, and who knows why a man should only want that in a wife? I shudder to think of life with someone who only likes the sight of me." She tossed her hair, removing a swarm of pins and letting her mane tumble free in thick blue-black waves. Tiger promptly started sweeping pins off the counter with his paw. Rowena didn't notice, still in mid-lecture. "If it's not for beauty, it's simply for utility. A wife is a commodity to most of the men in Cedar Point. Marriage means securing someone to cook, clean, warm their beds, and bear their sons."

"Mrowr?" Tiger thrust his head determinedly under her chin, purring. Was this comfort for his mistress, or mere pride because he'd managed to knock every single pin to the floor?

Rowena chose to believe the cat's actions were for her benefit.

"You're right," she mused, pretending that he'd said something beyond a happy mew. "There are a few who try to appeal to my intellect. Professor Trilby is certainly an accomplished man and a kind one…but I fear I'd be a widow not long after I was a bride. Tonight is the third time I've seen him reading as he walks home. He'll meet a messy end under the trolley if he's not careful."

Tiger hopped from the counter to the table, scattering the papers which bore the signature "Robert Mumford, Esq." With a bold swish of his opulent tail, he sent them soaring off the table.

"Tiger! You vain, infuriating thing. I need to edit those before tomorrow's post. Well…at least you didn't manage to spill the ink—this time."

A thoughtful frown settled on Rowena's beautiful face, which was gently rounded with pink, glowing cheeks and deep sky-blue eyes.

"You are vain and infuriating. You knock over the dustbins. You stole Mrs. Hill's salted cod. You knocked over Granny Nesbitt's peppermint oil and ruined her slippers." The frown turned to a thoughtful smile. "I dare say everyone in town knows what a menace you are."

Tiger gave his paw an insolent lick. It was only when he sat still and allowed you to really study him that one could see the black-on-black lines that ran through his coat. A black-striped tiger, a convenient household version.

"I don't like being alone, you know," Rowena murmured. A trace of the softness that she hid from most flowed easily around her confidant.

Tiger stopped his grooming ritual to take up his treasured post as Guardian of the Mumford Family, Nuzzler of Sad Cheeks, and Giver of Affectionate Nips. He rolled over onto his broad, black back and showed his tummy. As soon as Rowena stroked it, he wrapped his front paws tightly around her wrist and nibbled on her thumb.

"You're very sweet, and yes, I do have you. But it'd be nice to have someone human to chat with. Someone who likes to do the same things I do."

"Mrow?"

"Besides eating and sleeping, you naughty thing." Rowena gave the cat a solid scritch under the chin and freed her hand. "Work to do. Must get on." Any thoughts she'd had about ways to winkle out a potential mate from the horde of well-meaning (but boring) suitors vanished.

Chapter Two

Augustus Warwick leaned in the doorway of his shop. He loved this moment. Though the early spring meant longer days, the city of Cedar Point hadn't yet changed its nightly routine. At 7:00 Post Meridiem, on the nose, the tungsten electric streetlamp directly in front of Warwick's Whimsies flickered and flared to life. Each time, he let out an appreciative chuckle, which did not fully obscure his father's grunt of irritation.

"Should have left the old naphtha gas lamps. Why bother with this newfangled electricity in the street? You know it'll make the taxes go up."

"It's a very efficient light source, Father." Augustus walked back to his counter, leaving the door open, hopefully to invite courting couples and young married ones in, along with the soft April air. "Can you smell the lilacs? They've started blooming early this year. That good, warm snap we had."

His father answered with another grunt before taking his stick and hat in hand. "Good night, Augustus."

Augustus pushed his wayward tumble of auburn hair out of his eyes. "Oh. Good night, Father."

"Will you be coming home this evening?"

Warwick the Younger smothered a sigh. He had a flat above the store-cum-workshop. In the front, facing Main Street, was Warwick's Whimsies, the only confectioners in Cedar Point. In the back, facing

Turnbridge Alley, was Warwick's Bicycle and Instrument Repair. "Father, I am home."

"Not much of a home. No wife. No proper meals. No grandchildren to dandle on my knee."

"You never dandled an infant in your life. You had me marching to breakfast when I was three."

"I could have gotten you into West Point. You've got the brains, the bearing, the lineage..." Colonel Warwick, late of the Massachusetts Cedar Point 77th, Artillery Command, banged his stick on the floorboards as he limped toward the open door.

"Yes, I know." Augustus ended his comments there. He was tempted to launch into a litany of things he did not possess, things that were essential for a good soldier. Things that his father was not slow to remind him of when the mood struck him. But why argue?

Colonel Warwick paused, eye to eye with his son. Even in his sixtieth spring, the deep-blue orbs hadn't faded or lost their sharpness. "They would have fixed your hair for a start." His hand rose as if to brush back a buoyant lock from his son's forehead, then fell swiftly, ostensibly to fumble with his pocket watch.

"I doubt that. There are some things that not even the United States Army can save." Augustus tugged on his bangs, resistant to every sort of grease or pomade.

Colonel Warwick smiled in spite of himself. He might give his only son a hard time, but he loved the lad and wanted the best for him. It was hard for a military man of rigid views to understand how his son could turn down the glory, order, and *usefulness* of the military for a lifetime of making candies, pumping up rubber tires, and tuning people's pianos. "You should pop home. Your mother misses you." His voice dropped, no longer the stentorian tones that had terrified dozens of young cadets.

"I'll be home for Sunday supper, as always."

"Could bring a girl home, as well. Pretty enough lasses in town," the elder Warwick remarked, eyes squinting into the sunset.

Augustus barely contained a bray of laughter. What sort of girl would want Augustus Warwick, the man who constantly was letting the caramel burn, who was running about with a spanner sticking out of his trouser pockets, or was half-buried under a piano in a stranger's parlor? What sort of girl would want to be the wife of a man with graceless feet, nimble hands, and a brain that had no sense of timing? Why, at least four nights of the week, he woke up before first light, consumed with ideas for a new confectionary delight, and blundered down to the sweet shop kitchen in his pajamas.

Not to mention the hair.

Knowing that his father could keep silent indefinitely, Augustus cleared his throat and tried to explain why he would be showing up to dinner unaccompanied for the foreseeable future. "Yes, I know there are a number of beauties in town, but I—"

"Ah, well, at least your vision hasn't been totally obscured by that curly mop." His father gave a hearty laugh. "As I see it, you're well-placed for courting. You've got all the chocolates and sucking candies a woman could desire. Like catnip to a tabby! Must be a dozen girls in your shop each night." The colonel rubbed his hands together, warming to his clever idea.

"Yes. Easily." Augustus hesitated, then decided it was better to dash his father's hopes sooner rather than later. "But they're all being courted or already married."

"What, *all* of them?" Colonel Warwick clucked his tongue. It was clear from the frown beneath his walrus-like mustache that his boy just wasn't trying hard enough. "What about that…oh, what's her name? Clever girl? Parents died abroad a few years back?"

Augustus knew exactly who his father meant, but he refused to take the bait.

His father kept fishing. "Big house? Gives lessons in…some foreign language. She's eligible, wealthy, got a bit put by in the brains department—"

"Honestly, Father," Augustus hissed.

"Manford. Rowena Manford."

"*Mumford.*"

"Ah, you know her." His father's satisfied smile let Augustus know he'd been had.

"I have to tune her piano this week. She teaches piano, not 'some foreign language.' "

"She teaches French, too."

Augustus gaped at the smug-looking man before him, rocking on his highly polished bootheels. "How do you—"

"Your mother likes her. She said the other day that the poor thing was lonely. She's an odd woman, that Rowena. Pity, really, what with her being so pretty and the house being so big and empty."

As Augustus groped for a suitable reply, his father continued, mowing down any spluttering objections, just as his cannons would have mowed down the enemy.

"She's a strange woman, you're a…a…"

"Crackpot?" Augustus supplied with a soft groan.

"If you'd like. She must like sweets. Why don't you take her a box of those pink sugar things when you go to tune her piano?"

"Because—" Augustus took his father firmly by the elbow, his stumbling tongue replaced by solid reserve. "—that isn't how I would treat any other customer, and because Miss Mumford has no interest in any man in town, let alone the laughingstock of Cedar Point. Now—" He smoothed his apron, surprised at his own outburst. "—you'd best get home before Mother gets worried."

The old soldier sighed, his spine ramrod straight as he marched into the lavender-colored twilight. "You're very stubborn, boy!"

Augustus closed the door of Warwick's Whimsies and leaned on it, eyes to Heaven. "You couldn't have made him a bit more consistent, could You, Lord?"

No.

"No, I suppose not. You knew I wouldn't pray to You nearly as much if You had."

Chapter Three

"Miss Mumford. Another bunch of papers for Cincinnati?" Mr. Graves, the postmaster, smiled and took the bundle of sealed envelopes from Rowena's hand. All bore the elegant scrawl of *R. Mumford* in the corner and were addressed to James Peele, Editor, *Cincinnati Speculator.* "More charity appeals?"

"Ah. One or two." That was the truth. In addition to the articles and editorials she sent in as Robert Mumford, Esq., there was always an appeal for funds for the Pondicherry Orphanage, in India.

"Your father and mother would be so proud." Mr. Graves looked out from between steel-gray bangs and half-moon glasses. "I remember how often your mother led the Christmas bazaar and the chestnut roast by Beecher's Pond. You know, Mrs. Graves says the parish guild still needs ladies to help with the Easter festivities. Three weeks away."

"Ah. Yes." Rowena quickly handed over the coins required to purchase several of the green stamps adorned with Franklin's profile, china-blue lace gloves dipping into the small blue bag over her wrist. She might be the source of whispers among the little ones of Cedar Point, but that was no reason to be unfashionable. "I'll make sure to ask the minister's wife how I can be of assistance."

"You know, Mrs. Chambers was just in here for

some stationery for the Easter Invitational. The Mothers' League is—oh." The postman's kindly face dropped.

"Thank you, Mr. Graves. Will those go out on the noon train?"

"Absolutely, Miss Mumford."

****

Rowena hurried home. Carrie Earnshaw, one of the brightest girls in Cedar Point, was coming for French lessons. The French lessons were her ticket into Radcliffe, not that her parents were entirely thrilled with her desire to attend.

"Miss Mumford, how fortuitous." Professor Trilby bumped into her. Unlike some men, it wasn't a contrived "bump." The professor had been walking about with papers in front of his face, as usual.

"Professor. Thank you for your articles. I haven't gotten to read them yet, but I'm sure they're fascinating." Ever since Rowena had turned twenty, she had become quite adroit at fending off the casual overtures from prospective suitors before they even began.

"I would love to hear the opinions of an *educated* woman." Trilby bowed, nearly losing his glasses in the process.

"Indeed? Then perhaps you ought to show them to Miss Earnshaw as well, Captain Earnshaw's youngest daughter?" Rowena offered the girl's name as a test. Carrie Earnshaw was the daughter of one of Cedar Point's most respected pillars, Captain Earnshaw of the Cedar Point Ferry. The young lady was wonderfully intelligent. She was not exactly strikingly pretty, however.

To his credit, the professor looked eager. "Oh, I had not realized Miss Earnshaw was a 'college woman.' Did she attend your alma mater?"

"No, she is preparing to attend Radcliffe, as opposed to Oberlin, but I find her discussion most stimulating. She is quite fluent in French, as well."

"A sign of a skillful mind. Erm. Perhaps Miss Earnshaw would like to accompany you to a literary soiree some of my colleagues are hosting? A series of religious contemplations before Easter?"

"That does sound tempting, but—"

"Stop that mangy beast!"

Rowena stopped as Mr. Carver, the milkman, came tearing down the hill.

"Heavens!" Trilby jumped back, glasses slipping from his nose.

"Mr. Carver, what on earth?" Rowena gasped as the milkman, in his white apron, neat tie, navy waistcoat, and loose trousers, came streaking straight at them, a silver milk jug swinging wildly in his hand. When he realized that he was on a collision course with the elegantly dressed Miss Mumford and the professor, he slowed to a winded trot. It was only then that Rowena noticed a soggy black mass sprinting into the boxy hedges at the base of the hill.

"That blasted cat."

"Mind your tongue in front of the lady," Mr. Trilby admonished, stretching himself to his full, spindly height, his jaw jutting. This had the unfortunate side effect of dislodging his glasses (again). He struggled to reclaim them, ruining his protective efforts.

Rowena tried not to roll her eyes too obviously. "Tiger?"

"Miss Mumford, for the sake of Cedar Point's residents, you ought to keep him penned up inside the house. He's a big tom, too. Might get mistaken for a wildcat."

"Nonsense. There are no wildcats in Cedar Point," she said, voice even and eyes unblinking. "What has Tiger done this time?"

"He stuck his head into one of the big jugs. Ruined ten gallons." Mr. Carver clutched at his hat.

"Surely he didn't drink ten gallons of milk? He's big, but he's not *that* big," Rowena protested. This wouldn't be the first time Tiger had caused grief for Cedar Point's dairymen.

"No, but I can hardly sell it after a cat's stuck his head in it. Unhygienic." Mr. Carver gave a haughty sniff.

"I suppose you're right." Rowena sighed and opened her purse. "At fifteen cents a half gallon, and ten gallons spoiled, that'll be three dollars. I apologize, Mr. Carver. I hope your rounds won't be shorted." With a click of the clasp, she handed over the money.

Mr. Carver seemed nonplussed, shifting from foot to foot. "Accidents will happen." His flushed cheeks puffed out, eyes downcast. "But…half the milk is on the hillside, by now. Some is in the cart—the jug tipped over when I chased him out of it."

"Yes, I suppose I'm not getting what I paid for." Rowena glared at the bushes now rustling suspiciously.

"Quite! See here, Mr. Carver, the dairy can hardly expect a woman to pay for the carelessness of its employees. Who allowed the cat to sneak onto the cart?"

"That cat's in league with the devil. Oh, beggin' your pardon, Miss Mumford." Mr. Carver tugged his hat in apology, nodding to the beast's owner, but continued on the same track. "He's black as Lucifer and moves like a shadow despite his size. 'Tweren't anything careless about it."

"It's Tiger's fault that the milk was lost, wherever it remains. Give me the remainder, Mr. Carver. I'll strain it, boil it, and that should purify it enough to suit me." She forced a smile. She was going to be eating Granny Nesbitt's corn and clam chowder for a week straight. Oh, well. It was Tiger's favorite. He would certainly help eat the fruits of his disaster, even if he wouldn't help pay for it.

Mr. Carver was still standing in front of her, staring at the quarters in his palm as if they were the source of a toothache. "I...I'm..."

She had to smile. People like Mr. Carver, for all their bluster and bumble, were the reason she'd never stayed away from Cedar Point. The people were (with very few exceptions) generous and well-meaning. She could tell that after the milkman had calmed down, he was starting to feel sheepish, and something in the old manly pride didn't want to take the coins of a pretty spinster, living alone with her unruly cat.

Rowena surprised him, firmly reaching over and closing his fingers over the money. "You'd best be on your way, Mr. Carver. Your round must be nearly done. The mothers at the bottom of the hill will be waiting for you." With a gentle nudge of her fingers, she sent him blinking back to retrieve his cart, murmured apologies and goodbyes on both sides.

"Well. You handled that as well as any man, I must say," Professor Trilby gushed.

Rowena tried not to wince. It was meant as a compliment. Her mother's soft, cooing laugh tickled her memory. She recalled her whispered encouragement as Rowena had begun to capture the attention of the young men in town. *They don't know any better, dear. It's a unique man who can see the true strength of a woman before he's married to one.*

"I hope so. I don't think a woman's skills need be inferior to a man's. Simply different, and that is to say"—Rowena took a risk and spoke her mind, warming to the subject—"that women are so often educated and trained differently, treated differently, than men. If women were educated and trained in the same way as men, if they were treated as though they were capable of running a business or writing a scholarly paper…then the world would see. Women and men are different but quite equal."

Professor Trilby was staring at her with starry eyes, his weak chin dangling as his mouth dropped open.

He looked like a tall, pale grouper.

It was rather adorable. Rowena giggled.

"Miss Mumford. You are so…you are so stunningly pretty when you make an argument! Your cheeks flush like a tea rose. Your eyes—"

Her laughter died. Had he listened at all? Or had he been too busy looking? Disappointment anchored the lonely heart that had begun to lift slightly.

"You mustn't say such things," Rowena cut him off as he was making another long-winded simile about her beauty. "I must get on."

"Oh, but we haven't established what time I'm to arrive to escort you to the soiree." Professor Trilby followed her as she turned.

"I'll have to see if it's possible. I may have piano lessons that evening." Rowena sidestepped his fingers as they reached for her elbow. She didn't know when the literary evening was planned, but she had a fair number of piano students. There was a decent chance that their lessons were at least on the same night, even if not at the same time.

"Oh. Well, perhaps you and I could—"

Rowena and Trilby both stopped short, looking down.

Tiger sat between them, his face wet with milk and something gory. A dead sparrow, no longer intact, had been deposited on Professor Trilby's high-buttoned, neatly polished boots.

"What a *horrid* creature." Slender fingers whipped out a handkerchief and pressed it over his mouth, his pale skin turning a delicate green.

"Tiger is not a horrid creature. He is a protector. A companion. He's quite intelligent, as animals go. What's more, Professor Trilby, the gift of a bird or mouse isn't 'horrid' to the cat. It's the cat's way of showing you're important and worthy of attention."

"Or that the cat should be kept indoors where it can't harm innocent songbirds." Trilby frantically shook his trouser cuff.

"Come, Tiger," Rowena commanded, her voice cold enough to put frost on the budding lilacs.

Silky black tail held high, Tiger sauntered up the hill after his mistress.

****

Rowena tore off her wide-brimmed hat with its flutter of periwinkle netting. The gloves were next. She would gladly have shed her corset and run about in her cotton combinations, white cotton with eyelet embroidery on the sleeveless bodice and a double ruffle of almost translucent white fabric that swept to her knees.

But…that wouldn't do. Carrie Earnshaw would be over in a few hours, and the Thomas twins, Cedric and Harmon, would be there just after lunch. Not to mention the fact that there were about thirty glass bottles outside on the porch.

"You know, if they burn me at the stake, I'll blame you." Rowena glared at Tiger.

She'd have to haul out the big "cauldron" and invite Isabelle and her brood over for supper. "The whole house will stink of clams. No. No, I shall make a potato and corn chowder. Isabelle has a maid and a cook. Perhaps they'll attend to the clams?"

"Mrowr."

"Why in the world would you stick your head in the milk jug, you nuisance?" Rowena decided she'd change into a housedress at least. Perhaps if she wore something truly old and unflattering, the nightly parade of suitors would thin.

As she trotted down the stairs, now in a calico print of ivy on cream, she admonished, "And that poor bird, Tiger. And poor Trilby! You know, out of all of the men who drift by, he's the only one who tries to talk to me about 'academic' matters. Mr. Raine leers at me and thinks I'll find it charming. Mr. Ruger is clearly trying to fatten me up with the contents of his mother's larder. Pickles this week and an entire stollen the last. Heaven only knows what he'll bring me for Easter. Likely a suckling pig in a barrel of sauerkraut. What sort of dowry is that, I ask you?"

Tiger chased a small potato across the kitchen floor, losing it under the black-leaded stove. He flattened himself on his side and stuck his front paws underneath.

"Stop that. Just because you're already the color of

soot doesn't mean I want you to trail it all over the kitchen and into the parlor. Scat!"

Tiger reemerged, slinking low to the ground, trundling the potato along in front of him. It was now indistinguishable from one of the lumps of coal in the scuttle. With his sweeping tail, Tiger left a swipe of black against her dress and along the wall.

Rowena sighed as she shook out her skirt. "If you're trying to help Mr. Carver and Professor Trilby prove a point, you're doing a wonderful job."

Tiger jumped nimbly onto the piano bench, sooty paws marking the needlework seat. From there, he sat and stared at her, chrysoberyl eyes reproachful.

Although Tiger didn't "talk," Rowena often felt as though she understood his thoughts and replied to them out loud, simply for the comfort of conversation.

"Funny in the head," Granny Nesbitt had once assessed. "Grief does odd things to a person."

It wasn't grief that prompted her now, although once it might have been. "I'm angry about the milk. The bird was quite unnecessary. But—" Another sigh, this one deep and disappointed. "—I think the insight into Trilby's character was worth three dollars. If he pales and blusters at the normal behaviors of a pet...I shudder to think what he'd make of some of *my* behaviors."

That settled it. Tiger's habits, irritating though they were, were included in the matrimonial package. Idly playing a scale before she got down to the work of peeling potatoes and opening the jars of preserved summer corn, Rowena went over her "dowry" aloud, words tripping off her tongue in unison with her slim fingers striking the keys. "The chosen husband will receive a wife, beautiful of face, admirable of figure, talented, educated, wealthy, and *eccentric*." Chords cadenced underneath her final assets. "One large house. One excellent piano. One small pony cart (disused). One large, difficult feline."

Tiger jumped down and waited by the screen door.

"One…medical condition.

"The man that I marry must pass your test and mine." Rowena bent down and stroked the cat's ears. He regarded her with wide eyes, pupils mere slits in the sunny spot.

Rowena looked back. For a moment, her eyes seemed to match the stubborn feline's.

****

"Miss Mumford. Easter is coming." Mr. Ruger came up the gentle hill at sunset, leather boots clicking in time with his walking stick, carried for show, not for practicality's sake.

Well, honestly, she might be rumored to consort with the dark forces, but she was a God-fearing woman and a member of Cedar Point Episcopal. She *knew* that Easter was coming. "Indeed?" It was the only suitable reply she could muster.

Mr. Ruger took this as an invitation to discuss the coming holiday at length, including the traditions of his mother's family back in Germany.

Rowena nodded while wearing a polite smile and berating herself.

The dress hadn't worked. If anything, the sight of Miss Mumford dressed plainly seemed to inflame the local men.

They must envision me scrubbing their floors and ironing their shirts. This dress doesn't scream "woo me." It screams "wife," and that's worse.

I am a fool, education or not.

"Mother wants you to come to Easter luncheon. I want you to. Please. As my guest." Mr. Ruger offered a clumsy but heartfelt invitation, his bold blue eyes shining and his smile nervous.

"Oh, Mr. Ruger, how kind." Rowena smiled and pressed a hand to her heart. Mr. Ruger and his mother truly were lovely people. "You and your mother are such dear neighbors, but I'll be spending the day with my cousin Isabelle and her family."

"Perhaps another time? Mother would be delighted. O-or I would value your opinion on what sweets to buy my little nieces for Easter. The Osterhasen, you know?"

"The Osterhasen, Mr. Ruger?" Rowena's ears pricked up. It wasn't often that someone told her something she was wholly unfamiliar with. "What's that? What does it have to do with Easter?"

"In Germany, where my parents come from, it is the thing to do, to have the Osterhasen give gifts to families, mainly the children, after Lent. The women of the church pack up baskets wrapped in white linen, filled with all the things people give up, butter, cheese, meat, and sweets, oh, *the sweets*. The Easter Bunny, you would say, brings a basket full of those treats. Sometimes the ministers bless the baskets. We give them to the poor and elderly, too."

"Oh, Mr. Ruger, what a lovely thought. I hope the tradition takes root in Cedar Point."

"If Mother has anything to do with it, it will. She has already met with Mrs. Chambers, and the two of them are organizing an Easter Invitational, and the Mothers' League will use funds procured by the deacons and the parish guild to make baskets for all of the elderly and the children in the congregation, as well as those who are shut-in and infirm who can't attend."

Mr. Ruger was surely a fine, upstanding, and charitable man. Rowena felt a tug at her heart. Her late father and mother, who had been philanthropic to a fault, would have loved his idea. "I'm not a member of the Mothers' League, but I hope to help in some way."

"I'd be honored to have your assistance. Do you know—" He leaned closer, his mustaches bristling from the width of his smile. "—Mr. Warwick is keeping his sweet shop open until seven this spring? I could escort you there sometime, and you could help me select some samples. While we're there, we could try some of Mr. Warwick's specials ourselves. Have you had an 'ice cream cone'? They are all the rage in New York City."

"I have, Mr. Ruger." She laughed softly. "I am not quite so sheltered as that. A few newfangled things have made their way into my sphere. Why, I was even in New York City after the 1904 Louisiana Purchase Exposition. Ice cream cones were beginning to pop up all across the city." She blinked suddenly. That had been a happy trip, the last she and her parents had taken together. At the end of the trip, her parents had boarded the *SS Arabic* for Liverpool, and from there, they'd traveled to Calais, then through Europe to Pondicherry in India. Their journey had taken months. Rowena's had taken a day, via an express train from New York to Cleveland, and then a local stopping train to Oberlin and her final year of college.

They never returned.

If Mr. Ruger noticed the sudden sadness in her eyes, he mistook it for something else. "Don't fret, Miss Mumford," he murmured, daring to pat the hand that held her gleaming tin watering can.

"Pardon?" Rowena shook herself, startled by his touch and the abrupt departure from her memories.

"One day, I feel sure that you will be welcomed into the Mothers' League. I—ahem. Well. Some night soon, we will go to the sweet shop, yes?"

"Yes?" she blurted in response, still taken aback by his comment about her future motherhood.

"Wonderful! Good night." Mr. Ruger swaggered off, almost clicking his heels in delight. Doubtless his dinner table conversation would include news that he had persuaded the unpersuadable Miss Mumford to accompany him to Warwick's Whimsies for an ice cream.

Oh dear.

Well, that clinched it. She would have to put her plan into action.

Chapter Four

Cedar Point was a "dry town." Saloons and taverns didn't exist within the city limits. A small billiard parlor offered cigars and pipe tobacco accompanied by sarsaparilla, soda water, tonic and lime, and cider made from the stubborn, tart green apples of Harwood's Orchard. However, Pinkerton's Billiards was a seedy establishment that most of the "upstanding" men of Cedar Point wouldn't be seen in. In a small town, gossip ran like the streetcar, morning, noon, and night, with stops at either end of town.

Augustus Warwick knew (as well as everyone else in town) that "respectable wines" and "medicinal" liquors were kept in cabinets and flasks in many homes. But, since most of the young, unmarried men didn't want to sit inside and ruminate over a glass of port or skulk outside a smoky billiard room, Warwick's Whimsies was fast becoming a post-work, predinner gathering spot.

Augustus was kept busy supplying penny candies to the schoolchildren who stopped on their way home, and then phosphates and ice cream sodas to the "suits and shopkeeper set," as he'd come to think of them.

Three prime examples of this population came in now, voices hearty as they dominated the entryway.

"Never, Ruger."

"It's true, Trilby."

"You're both half-mad with thirst. Warwick, three cherry phosphates."

"Of course, Matthew." Augustus had gone to school with all three of the men who were perching against his gleaming glass countertop. Matthew Raine had been the most handsome boy and the richest one. His parents owned both the paper and lumber mills. Wolfie Ruger had moved into town later, when his father bought the tailor's shop after the old owner retired. Simon Trilby, who'd always marched along in his father's footsteps, was now a professor at the nearby seminary, just as his father had been.

It was funny to see those three faces staring back at him from the other side of the counter, talking away, deep in a conversation that he wasn't privy to.

I prefer my own company too much, the tinkering and the tasting, living in a world of my own senses, Augustus thought as he watched the foam fizz and bubble in three tall glasses, stirring in the cherry syrup he brewed in the shop's kitchen.

"I'm not the one who's mad, Matthew. You're the one who's insane, waiting for so long to make a bold move."

"I brought her flowers only yesterday. The hussy accepted." Raine's handsome features twisted in a scowl of distaste.

"I say, Matthew. That's unkind and unworthy of you. She's not a hussy or anything of the sort for accepting your bouquet," Simon Trilby rebuked in his thin, reedy voice.

Ah. Rowena Mumford, the belle of Cedar Point. Augustus tried to ignore the conversation, but found himself drawn in. Of course, there were other customers in the shop, young couples who were courting, for the most part. As he took their orders and smiled at all the young love in the air, he couldn't help but catch snatches of conversation.

"—Easter luncheon. Then, we were talking about the Osterhasen—"

"What, Ruger? Some German custom?"

"If you'd bothered to spend more time learning your Latin and German than parting your hair, Raine!"

Augustus smothered a laugh. Trilby had always been the tiniest lad in the school, but he strode about like Goliath, confident that his brains would outlast and outwit any brawn.

"She all but agreed to attend a symposium with me. She's heading to Warwick's with Wolfie. It looks like *you're* the only one who hasn't got a horse in this race, Matthew. Forcing a bunch of wildflowers into a girl's hand hardly counts as wooing, if you ask me. What do you say, Wolfgang?"

"I agree, Simon. May the best man win."

With boisterous laughs, the broad, mustachioed Ruger and the pale, spindly Trilby shook hands across a sulking Matthew Raine.

Serves Raine right, thinking any woman he wants will fall at his feet. Augustus hummed to himself as he scooped chocolate-covered peanuts into a little white bag.

His smile of satisfaction shifted into a tight frown. Merged with the smile he tried to keep in place for customers, he must look quite menacing, grimacing at all of them.

But why should the courtship of Miss Mumford be considered some sort of sporting event? Some foxhunt?

Any moment now, he wouldn't be surprised if Matthew Raine pulled out his ever-bulging wallet and—

The slap of cowhide on glass made him turn.

"Five dollars, gentlemen. Five dollars to the man who places a ring upon her finger first."

"Good heavens, engagement? Matthew, no one has even had the pleasure of taking her for a walk by the lake," Trilby squawked.

After a moment of thoughtful frowning, Ruger tapped the counter. "I'll take your bet, Raine. The money will go to the missionary fund when I win."

"It will go to the seminary scholarship fund if *I* win." Trilby warmed to the idea.

Raine rolled his eyes. "If I win, it'll go to a nice, fat honeymoon."

The leer on Raine's face made Augustus want to shove the silver scoop from the nut barrel up the man's nose. Maybe it would smack into his brain and jar it back into working order.

"An additional term, gentlemen," Trilby proposed, voice dropping.

The crowd thinned out. It would surge again after dinner, before all the respectable folk of Cedar Point went home to sit on their porches or play cribbage in their parlors. Augustus watched a giggling redhead pawing her beau's arm as he balanced a bonbon on her nose. Over the soft tittering, he could hear almost every word of the trio finishing their drinks.

"It must occur by the end of spring. The engagement must be announced before the Fourth of July at the very latest, if not sooner." Trilby raised a priggish forefinger in the air as if addressing a roomful of rowdy pupils.

"What? Good heavens, Simon. Ever since the girl's

parents died, let me see, six years ago, was it? Well, ever since then, no one has persuaded her to even go on a walk or join them at the annual clambake. You suddenly want us to sway her to matrimony in a matter of weeks?" yelped Raine, his slicked bangs escaping in his agitation, falling in a curly wave over his brow.

"Why the rush? It wouldn't look proper." Mr. Ruger sucked viciously on the straw inside his glass, mustache flexing and fluttering on every sip.

"Because, gentlemen, after July fifth I shall be filling the pulpit at a Cape Cod chapel for the remainder of the summer. I agreed to take the post so an old seminary chum can take his wife west to get some dry heat into her lungs. She had consumptive pneumonia over the winter."

"Shame. Shame. Well, that's all fair and good, Trilby. But still, just because you've a mind to be a ministering angel, I don't see why we have to put a deadline on ourselves." Matthew Raine allowed several copper coins to roll across the counter. "Another one. Blackberry, please, Warwick."

"Of course. Simon? Wolfgang? The same again?" Augustus asked, grateful for the chance to get closer.

"Another cherry." Trilby nodded.

"I'll try the blackberry." Ruger placed coins of his own alongside Matthew's.

"There has to be a deadline, or else we cannot begin this silliness until I return in the fall. I shall be out of the running for the summer. If you two are still here, pressing your suits upon her, then you'll have an unfair advantage. If she won't accept any of us by July, then the bet is off, and we can make a new one upon my return. Do I have your word as gentlemen, gentlemen?"

Augustus decided that he absolutely had to go out to the icebox in the back of the shop and smash one of the smaller blocks to bits, and he had to do it right now. "I'll be back with your drinks in a moment, fellows," he grunted, picking up a hammer on his way into the dark.

****

Augustus woke up in his bedroom, sunlight skewering him in the eyes. He must've fallen asleep with the curtains not quite drawn. For a moment, he lay there, wondering what was out of place or wrong in his universe.

His father hadn't nagged him yesterday.

He had turned a tidy sum in the shop.

The bicycle he'd been working on was repaired and due to be delivered. He had all day to tinker in the workshop and work in the kitchen of the "confectionary," as he liked to think of it.

Tomorrow morning, he had to pay a call on Rowena Mumford and Temple Israel, the synagogue just outside of Cedar Point.

Rowena Mumford.

A pretty girl, very sweet and very shy. He remembered that Tobias Swanson once dunked her beautiful black braid in an inkwell, and no one even noticed until she walked to the front of the school room, leaving a trail of glistening mussel-black drops.

She was a grade or two behind him in school, but they didn't mix. By the time he had started to grow curious about the family, and maybe even notice what a beautiful daughter they had, Rowena and her family were off, traveling in Europe. Rowena went to music school in Paris, they said, and studied at a ladies' finishing school in London. She went to college in the

States, one of the first women in Cedar Point to attend an institute of higher learning, shocking many of the older ladies in town. Rumors swirled about the younger Miss Mumford, but Augustus and his family had little interest in rumors.

So why, suddenly, could he only think about the gossip he'd overheard last night? Gossip that didn't concern him. Gossip that was nonsensical. If Miss Mumford wanted to get married, let her.

"She's too smart to fall for anything...insincere," Augustus muttered, scraping his hair back from his forehead. The bangs simply unfurled, looking as if he'd never touched them.

With a groan, he hurried and got ready for the day, hoping that he'd have a few quiet hours in the kitchen to work whatever was ailing him out of his system.

No such luck.

He'd barely gotten started on the usual daily requirements—roasting nuts, making the flavored syrups for phosphates and the cake batter for his petit fours (he could hear his father groaning from the other side of town)—when the bell above the door tinkled.

"Ah, Mrs. Chambers, Mrs. Ruger, come in." Augustus dried his hands on his canvas apron, which was covered in equal amounts of chocolate and axle grease. "The shop isn't open yet, but—"

"We know. We wanted your undivided attention, Young Mr. Warwick." Mrs. Chambers beamed at him and bustled over.

Mrs. Chambers was tiny, barely five-feet, but she had an air of suppressed energy, like a stallion endlessly pawing the ground, waiting to run. It made her seem taller somehow, with an aura of bright energy trembling around her, ready to set itself on a task. Her brown hair was shot through with wispy silver threads and held back in an enamel clasp. Out of all the residents in Cedar Point, she was the only one who persisted in calling him "Young Mr. Warwick," even when his father was nowhere in sight.

"Well, ladies, you may have it." Augustus bowed slightly to each of the matrons before him, pushing down the urge to tell Mrs. Ruger that her son was gambling on a lady's virtue. (Which was a stretch, but Augustus was still fighting off the nameless irritation he'd woken up with.) "How may I assist you? Is it the church organ again?"

"No, it isn't your piano repair skills we are after." Mrs. Ruger, as tall and broad as her son but much rounder, plopped a newspaper in front of him.

Augustus peered at it, wondering if he'd had a funny turn in the night. He couldn't read the words. "Ah…yes?"

"This is from my sister in Germany. You see the advertisements, yes?" Mrs. Ruger tapped the paper. "It is for Easter, you see? This here, this is telling the men they can get a new suit for Easter, and this is a sale on ladies' hats."

The shopkeeper nodded, bewildered. "I've seen that in our papers, too." There were endless advertisements for spring clothes, spring frocks, hats, shoes, parasols, and a dozen other things in the *Cedar Point Register.*

"But your papers do not have the Osterhasen," Mrs. Ruger said smugly, a wide smile on her face as her arms crossed over her abundant bosom. She tapped an illustration of a basket filled with bread, candy, and fruit. "Baskets of treats to give to the children and the elderly."

"Well, the baskets will be full of more nourishing items, given to the elderly, sick, and poor among us," Mrs. Chambers interposed. "But for the children in the congregation…we'd like your help. We want a bag of sweets. Something bright and pretty. Something that won't stain their clothes—"

"No chocolate!" Mrs. Ruger thundered.

"Bright, colorful, nonstaining, and non-chocolate treats?"

"Something with a variety of flavors would be nice," mused Mrs. Chambers, her white-gloved fingers thoughtfully caressing her chin.

"And you will be compensated. Of course…it is for the children."

"A discount can be arranged." He smiled. He would have done that anyway. Children were some of his very best customers, and garnering goodwill with their parents was always welcome.

"Oh, and the candies shouldn't be hard. The little ones, you know. They might break their teeth on those hard-boiled sweets."

"Ah. Let me write this down." Augustus grabbed a pad of paper and pen off of the back counter and scribbled the requirements.

Soft and easily chewed
Colorful
Different flavors
No chocolates
Small

"Do you think you can supply something for us, Young Mr. Warwick?"

"For how many children?"

"Oh…two hundred, I expect?"

He paled and then shook himself. "You don't need these soon, do you?"

"No, no. You could even bring them with you to Easter service if you'd like. I know you have that little cart attached to your bicycle."

"Of course. I'll bring them with me on Easter Sunday. I'll draw up an agreement and drop it off at the manse." Augustus gave the ladies a charming smile.

"What do you think you'll be making, Mr. Warwick?" asked Mrs. Ruger.

"Oh...something whimsical." Augustus bowed, hoping they would take the hint.

They did, chatting as they made their way from the store.

Thank heavens. Augustus slumped against the counter, head propped in his hands as his elbows framed the list.

Something whimsical. In other words...I haven't the faintest idea!

Chapter Five

Carrie Earnshaw sat at the table for the second time that week. But this time, the girl wasn't eagerly conjugating French verbs or talking about her acceptance to Radcliffe. This time, she sported a grim look that added tension to her already plain face.

While Rowena thought her pupil had a sort of austere attractiveness, the frown didn't help matters. "Carrie? What's wrong, dear?"

The girl seemed to be having a brief inner struggle, but then the words rolled out, half-choked and riddled with tears. "Oh, Miss Mumford, it's shameful. It's utt-utterly shameful!"

"What? What's shameful?" Rowena's heart immediately skipped a beat. *Who knew? Who found out, and how?*

"My brother works at Raine's paper mill."

Rowena blinked and slowly took a seat across the parlor table, patting her pupil's hand. "Now, Carrie! That's nothing to be ashamed of. It's Charles, isn't it? Charles is a bright boy and a hard worker. The paper mill is a suitable, honest job. It may not be elegant, but—"

"No, Miss Mumford. H-he heard Mr. Raine telling his father, the older Mr. Raine, that he needs time away from the mill for his honeymoon in Europe! The fashionable people go to Paris for their wedding trips, you see."

"Oh, Carrie." Rowena scooted her chair around and placed her arm around Carrie's shaking shoulders. "You had feelings for Matthew Raine? He's very attractive, I'll admit, and yes, some would even find him charming. But you shouldn't fret over his engagement to another girl, my dear. I honestly don't think you'd be well suited. For one thing, your brilliance would far outshine his. I doubt he'd fully appreciate your wit, your charm, your...*intelligence*."

Carrie stared, her pale lips forming a confused burst of surprise. "But, I don't think I'm anywhere near as intelligent as you. Perhaps one day after I've completed my education..." The girl trailed off.

"I do not believe the good Lord intends for us to compare ourselves to one another." Rowena prayed that her pupil would not turn to physical comparisons next. She had the feeling that she was failing at being a sisterly confidant and comforter. Rowena wished for the millionth time that her mother was still alive to give out pearls of wisdom.

Carrie wiped her eyes on the long, tight-fitting sleeves of her dress. "Nor do I, Miss Mumford. Only, if you think Matthew Raine won't appreciate *my* intelligence, then I feel he would scarcely appreciate yours."

"Mine?" Rowena repeated, brows drawing together. "Why am I involved in this?"

Carrie's hazel eyes widened. "Why, you're the one he's going to marry! At least, that's what he told his father."

"Preposterous."

"It's not true? I must say, I *am* glad. I don't want to be disrespectful to my brother's employer, and I know the Raines are a fine family, and I'm sure Matthew Raine would make a wonderful husband…But as you said, I didn't think he would value your intelligence. On the few occasions I've had the opportunity to meet him, he only talks about himself and his own prospects."

"That is very astute of you, Carrie," said Rowena, her heart flying once again, this time with a different kind of terror. What would possess Matthew Raine to make such a bizarre claim? Surely the acceptance of a single bouquet of flowers from a passing gentleman did not equal a betrothal.

"I wish I knew exactly what your brother had overheard," said Rowena, trying to sound calm. "Perhaps he misunderstood?"

"Perhaps," Carrie freely admitted, "I'm certain that must be it. I must have gotten my wires crossed, as my father would say."

"Yes, that must be it. Well then"—Rowena forced a note of gaiety into her voice as she patted the girl's shoulder—"there's no harm done. I've no intention of marrying Matthew Raine. Why, he hasn't even asked me to! The only person who's asked me to accompany him anywhere is Mr. Ruger, who wants my assistance with some charity work. Oh, and Professor Trilby, who would like me to attend some intellectual soiree as his guest. You know, Carrie. He is a man who truly appreciates intelligence. He is just the sort of man I think we both should look for, should we ever feel the desire to do the pursuing and not simply wait around for the wooing." Rowena nodded firmly, rather pleased with her own turn of phrase.

"He spoke at the school around Christmas on the meanings of the sacred carols. I was very moved." Carrie nodded, eyes dreamy. "But he must be close to your age."

Rowena stifled a grimace. She was only a few years older than Carrie! "He's around my age, and an established man can be a blessing for a young woman. I think you ought to match wits with him sometime and see if he's the sort of man you'd enjoy spending time with...Provided you don't keep a cat." Her blue eyes flashed with a sudden burst of anger.

Carrie missed it, blowing her nose in a handkerchief retrieved from the cuff of her sleeve. "Oh no, Father has a cat aboard the ferry, but I like dogs better. Not that cats aren't wonderful things. Father says they're very useful, and no ship should be without one."

"I quite agree," said Rowena, "cats are wonderful, useful creatures. They...they may help me solve a bit of a problem, a problem that some women wouldn't even consider a difficulty."

"Oh? What's that, Miss Mumford?"

"Call me Rowena, Carrie. If we are going to talk about the problems modern, educated women face, then we should treat each other as friends, friends who learn from one another."

The younger girl looked like she might burst, squirming suddenly in her seat before composing herself and trying to look worldly and womanly. "You are right as always, Mi—Rowena."

"You see, I think a lot can be learned about the character of a man based on how he treats the less powerful beings in his life."

"Which sadly includes women?" Carrie hazarded.

Rowena nodded. "I hadn't even...Yes, Carrie, you're correct. But I meant cats. Cats like Tiger, who have a reputation for mischief and mayhem. All of the town knows him. Half avoid him, half chase him with a broom."

"Poor Tiger. That seems unfair. He's very clever."

"Quite. Too clever for his own good." Rowena looked at her beloved pet again. He stretched in the sun, rolled over, and went back to sleep, the bright golden light highlighting the black-on-black pattern of his stripes. "Carrie—" She turned back to the girl and impulsively took both of her hands. "—I don't believe Matthew Raine is the only man who makes presumptions about me or my matrimonial state. I'm…I'm not averse to marriage. I'm simply averse to the way the men in Cedar Point go about wooing. It's all a lot of courtly show, calling round with flowers and pickles."

"Pickles?" Carrie repeated, confused.

"Never mind that. It's hard to find a man who you would live with, who would accept you, warts and all. People are always on their best behavior while they woo…and yet it seems the problems start after they wed." Rowena winced, remembering some of the rather spectacular tantrums she'd witnessed Cousin Isabelle throw. Thank heavens her husband was a patient, solid sort of man.

"I agree. But, how does the cat enter in, Rowena?" Carrie pressed.

"Tiger…Tiger was a gift my grandmother gave me when my parents passed and I returned to Cedar Point. She wanted me to stay with her, not live in this house all alone. When I was resolute about keeping on living in the family home, she gave me Tiger, as a kitten. I wouldn't part with him."

"Of course not. Nor should any man ask you to."

Carrie crossed her arms over her narrow chest, jaw clenched.

"I have a feeling some men might ask exactly that." Rowena mirrored the girl's stance. "So, let it be known now that any man who wishes to court me will have to prove himself first."

The younger woman's eyes were suddenly aglow with excitement, her hands changing from a defiant cross to an eager clasp. "Like Tennyson and Mallory! A quest to...well, I suppose you couldn't really send them to slay a dragon, could you?"

Rowena silently turned to the piano in the parlor corner and opened a delicate china box that had been Grandma Mumford's. She retrieved a polished silver bell, covered in elegant scrolls, dangling from a silver filigree chain. "No, there will be no literal dragons to slay, Carrie, dear. Just one *Tiger*. Whoever can put a bell around his troublemaking neck may call upon me and be assured that I'll listen to his suit." Her blue eyes darkened as she stood in the dim corner, pupils wide. "That's an offer I've never made. Any man ought to be grateful for the chance."

"That's a splendid plan!" Carrie paced around the table where books and papers were spread, the swish of her skirts audible in the silent house. "Miss Mumford, you are clever. Even Father says so."

"Does he?" Rowena gave the girl a small smile. "High praise." Captain Earnshaw wasn't a man given to talk, idle or otherwise. If he had taken the trouble to mention her name in a complimentary way, that meant a great deal.

"Indeed. Father even said—" Carrie took a gulping breath. "—that if a 'smart woman like Rowena Mumford believes our Carrie can make it at some fancy women's college, then I think so, too, by Neptune's beard!' Oh, not that Father is a pagan, Miss Mumford."

"No, Carrie, well do I know that. Simply a son of the sea. And you must call me Rowena, dear."

"Rowena, you're far smarter than I am, but I'm afraid I've found a flaw in your plan. Once the infatuated beaus around town hear about the bell, Tiger will be hunted like a prime stag. The men will be after him with nets and things." Carrie twisted her hands as she paced on the blue-rust-and-bronze-colored Persian rug that adorned most of the parlor floor. "They might even hurt him."

Rowena kept her back to the girl, her eyes fixed on the portrait above the mantel. Her mother and father smiled down in oils, her mother's eyes the exact same shade of blue as hers, her raven hair Rowena's twin. Even in lifeless paint, it was clear her father utterly adored his wife. "The right man won't do any such thing."

"It's the *wrong* men I'd worry about," Carrie muttered darkly as she held her ground, spine stiff and fists on her hips. "The ones who might get to Tiger first."

"Oh…Don't worry too much about Tiger. They say a cat has nine lives, after all." Rowena slipped the bell and chain back in the box. "Now. We *must* get some French done before you have to leave."

Carried sighed, then smiled. "I think I'll take Charles some sandwiches at the mill. He has a fierce appetite." Her eyes twinkled as Rowena turned back to her. "He's a wonderful brother, Rowena. Always so thoughtful. He always asks after my studies. I'll have to tell him about the interesting conversation we had."

"But discreetly!" Rowena advised, stomach suddenly squirming in nervousness. What if the plan failed? What if it worked? She didn't know which idea terrified her more.

Carried nodded firmly, her sharp chin set. They shared a conspiratorial smile. "Discreetly, Rowena."

Chapter Six

"What in the name of Sainted Abraham Lincoln are you doing with all of those smashed fruits?" Colonel Warwick poked his stick at the counter where Augustus had colanders of strained strawberries, peaches, spinach, and heaven knew what else.

"I'm making jelly eggs," Augustus replied as he slid a flat white handkerchief over his brow and tied it, tired of doing battle with his wayward bangs.

"Pickled eggs?" Warwick the elder harrumphed.

"No," Augustus said from between gritted teeth. "Jelly eggs. I'm setting them with gelatin in the mixture, Father, and then they harden. At least that's the idea—a cross between a jellied sweet and a boiled sweet, I'd say."

"What the devil for?" Warwick Senior demanded, now thumping his cane on the scuffed wooden floor, which needed a mopping before the customers began to trickle in. "The place looks like a greengrocer's exploded. Haven't you got enough to do without inventing *another* confection to rot the teeth of the children in this town?"

"You're in a foul mood." Augustus was too tired to mince words. He'd been up half of the night and again early this morning, feeling pressure to perfect the sweets before Easter week. He figured that he'd need a week to perfect the recipe and then a week or two to make enough

42

for the church, on top of everything else he had in his already heavily scheduled life. Foul mood or not, his father could be right about one thing—a wife might be a useful thing to have. His father wanted him to wed in order to show the town that his only son wasn't *only* a crackpot dreamer and candymaker, that he was also somewhat normal. But Augustus was realizing that a wife might be an invaluable help right about now. On top of the endless whirl of sweets, pianos, and bicycles in his brain, now Augustus' heart decided to give a longing thump.

The older man stood at attention, facing away from his son. "I'm in no such mood. You're simply cranky because you're not being looked after properly. Why don't you rent out the flat to one of those young clerks at the bank and move back home?"

"Because you and I would drive each other mad inside of a week, and Mother wouldn't like it," Augustus said, chuckling a bit at the end. From the other side of the counter, he heard his father try (and fail) to smother the same sound.

"I suppose there is some truth to that," Colonel Warwick admitted. "No, I'm not in a foul mood, son. It's just that…Well, your mother has it in her head that her only son deserves a June wedding."

"Isn't that for brides?" Augustus remarked, stirring vigorously at the stove.

"Well, if there's a bride, there must be a groom somewhere in the mix," the colonel pointed out dryly. "No, my boy, it's just that she started on again this morning. If you haven't found a girl at the beginning of spring, there's certainly no hope for a summer wedding. I tried to tell her it's not so. You're older now and more settled." He fixed Augustus with a fish-eyed stare. "Settled after a fashion, that is. I suppose there might be some older women who would be ready to move to the altar with haste, who wouldn't take much wooing. Or some of the young ladies without a beau. They might think you're a catch. Good family. Decent income you could draw on, not to mention all of your *business ventures*. You ought to snag one of those pretty young things looking for a man who can bring a bit of security. And you're nearly thirty. That's a good age for a younger wife. You are successful. In a loose way."

"Oh, please, not one more backhanded compliment. I simply can't take it." Working with a sudden frenzy, Augustus dumped out a pink mixture that smelled like summer fruits. He spread it on a long sheet of greaseproof paper. Using the edge of a buttered knife and the paper together, he rolled the mixture into a thin log. Catching the sound of the church clock chiming the hour, Augustus suddenly gasped and turned to another log, this one black and resting on the front counter. With a sharp knife, he cut the log into tiny pieces and rolled each one into the shape of an egg no bigger than his thumbnail.

"There. Jelly eggs!" Augustus proclaimed in satisfaction.

His father watched it all with his gray, tufted eyebrows rising to meet his hairline and his bristling mustache temporarily at rest. "I doubt you should call these 'jelly eggs,' Augustus. Looks more like wet licorice drops to me."

"They won't all be licorice," Augustus protested. "I've got some strawberry ones cooking and some mint straining, and I've just made a batch of peach and cherry. I think they'll be delicious."

"Delicious they may be, but eggs they are not. Why in the world would you call them 'eggs'? Is this another one of your whimsies, boy?" Sharp eyes narrowed and peered at the row of tiny ovals.

"It's spring and Resurrection, Father. Think of the chicks hatching and the baby birds in the nest." Augustus gestured vaguely into the outside world where spring had come to Cedar Point. "Think of them as robin's eggs."

"Very titchy little robins." Colonel Warwick snuck a gleaming black bead from the counter and popped it into his mouth. "I say you ought to call them 'jelly beans' if you're going to call them jelly anything."

"Beans are not very spring-like." Augustus popped one of the black licorice sweets into his mouth and smacked his lips. "It's a very good batch. Mild but tangy enough." Inwardly, he supposed black wasn't very spring-like, either. He might have to leave these out of the Easter arrangements. What's more, he was sure his father would have the same argument.

"Black licorice is hardly a bastion of spring," argued the colonel. "And what do you mean, beans aren't associated with spring? That's the first thing up in your mother's garden every year, crocuses and runner beans."

"These were not my idea," Augustus finally snapped. "The church wants me to make these for the Easter baskets they're giving the children in the congregation and throughout town."

"Easter baskets?"

"Ask Mrs. Chambers." Augustus leapt back to the stove as the bubbling red liquid reached the top of the large metal pot.

"Ah. For the church, is it? Well. That's a good thing. Your mother will be pleased."

"Thank heavens. Something I do pleases someone," Augustus mumbled. "Did you want to talk about anything besides my matrimonial plans?"

"Not much else to be said. I'm on my way to the bank. I'll see you soon."

Before Augustus could even make a reply, his father had disappeared out of the door.

He sagged. Another hour before the shop opened, although he'd have to close it in the afternoon to attend to Miss Mumford's piano.

Good. Calm before the storm.

****

Augustus had no idea how apt the phrase "calm before the storm" would prove to be. He'd no sooner changed into a clean white apron over his brown check waistcoat and starched shirt when half of the single men in Cedar Point burst into his shop.

Matthew Raine was at the head of the pack, a wad of bills in his hand. "Say, Warwick, you sell bells, don't you?"

"Bells?" Augustus blinked.

"Bells! The small silver sort, the ones you put on boys' bicycles," Raine demanded, impatience in his tone.

"Well…yes. But the repair shop is around the back, this is the—"

"I'm not after a repair. I want to buy a bell. Now nip into the back and fetch one."

"Fetch two!"

"Fetch the whole case!" called a voice in the back of the throng, earning uproarious laughter.

Curious though he was, profit was profit. Augustus hurried to the back of the sweet shop and through the clutter of his workshop, stepping over spanners and air tubes. He had a box of bells, some that jingled and swayed, some that had a tiny lever on the side that struck a silver dome and made a metallic *ting* when released. Augustus usually sold one or two a month. By the look of the line in front of his counter, he'd be selling about thirty in an hour.

As soon as he returned to the candy counter, the crowd of men began to push and shove, laughing and shouting as if they were all off on some great adventure. Perhaps they were all about to start cycling around town. He'd heard it was becoming a more popular pastime, especially in warm weather. "You've all caught bicycle fever, gentlemen?" Augustus said when the crowd had thinned a little. In a flurry of money and silver, he finally made himself heard.

"Can't have that kind." Horace Canby, the fishmonger's assistant, pushed aside the bells with levers. "Where are the sort that jingle? The ones they sew onto the harnesses of the horses who march in the parade?"

"Sleigh bells?"

"That'll do. Matthew Raine got that kind. I saw him."

"Those aren't as popular on bicycles. You might want to try the livery. Or the tinker? Maybe even at Ostlemeyer's?" Augustus mentioned the local blacksmith with growing confusion.

"I'll have to go after work. But I'm not worried." Horace left with a jovial wink. Several of the men departed with him, while a few stayed and asked Augustus for some of his wares.

"That young Canby thinks *he's* in with a chance," scoffed one. "A pound of peanut brittle, Augustus."

Augustus complied with his customer's request. He knew the man, just like he knew nearly everyone in Cedar Point, but he couldn't quite place him. It was one of the Fulham brothers (and there were quite a few), who owned the feedstore. "Of course, Mr. Fulham."

"It doesn't matter if he gets his way round the cat," one of Fulham's companions said brightly. "Say what she might, she'll have nothing to do with that young sprout. He's only eighteen."

Cat. She. Augustus handed the peanut brittle back in a striped bag and took the next order, a strawberry phosphate. "Are you...buying a lady a bell for her bicycle, Mr. Fulham?"

"Oh, you haven't heard? Warwick, you'd best get in on this!"

"Shush, George, no use asking Warwick to take notice of this situation. He wouldn't have a chance." The other man, one of the clerks at the bank, gave Augustus a pitying smile. "That is, this sort of thing wouldn't interest you."

Augustus knew he could look imposing when he wanted to, and right now he wanted to. He hated being mistaken for a dullard or an unambitious man simply because he was an *unusual* man. He had failed to fit the Cedar Point or West Point mold, but that didn't mean he had no civic pride, no community interest. Fixing the pair of customers with his lips in a grim, thin line, he drew himself up to his just over six-foot stature and flared his shoulders back.

Fulham started talking immediately. "Rowena Mumford, Augustus. She's finally ready to think of marriage. Or at least, ready to think of courting! She and that blasted big tomcat she calls a pet are inseparable, you know. Thing should have been drowned in a bucket the first time it nicked a piece of haddock out of the fishmonger's."

"And the bell?" Augustus glowered.

Fulham leaned in, whispering. "Any man who can bell that cat will be considered a worthy suitor. The first step on the road to the altar, you see."

"Whose idea was that?" Augustus had to ask, torn between admiration at the creativity and worry that poor Miss Mumford (whom he felt a special kinship for, despite barely knowing her) would soon be overwhelmed with a pack of men stalking through her garden.

"Well, Carrie Earnshaw, who takes French from Miss Mumford, told her brother Charles, who works under Matthew Raine at the mill. Matthew Raine told the foreman at the mill, who rooms with Mrs. Hudson, who—"

"Has the ablest tongue in town. Yes. Well, it's a clever idea. I only hope she knows what she's getting herself into." He managed to hide his frown. The idea of Matthew Raine, always impeccably dressed, scrounging around in the tall grass trying to catch the big black cat was laughable. His lips quirked. The idea of Horace Canby luring the cat with a fresh-caught flounder pasted the grimace on again. "Why would any man want to enter this 'contest'?" he mused aloud.

It was a mistake. He rarely spoke. His ideas weren't popular among the local men of his age.

"Why *wouldn't* he? Rowena Mumford is pretty, wealthy, and far from old. She'll make a man a fine wife and mother." The clerk slurped his drink, leaving a dot of foam on the corners of his thin, waxed mustache.

"Will she? Tell me, Mister…"

"Cobb. Owen Cobb, Mr. Warwick." Cobb gave him a chilly stare, as if annoyed that a common candymaker wouldn't remember the name of a man in *banking*, however lowly.

"Cobb. What sort of thing would you talk to Rowena Mumford about every evening?"

Cobb laughed, blinking in shock. "Why, things about the house. I'm sure she'll have news from her sewing circle and whatever else she gets up to."

Music. French. And…Augustus couldn't quite recall the details, but he knew Rowena wrote or did something in the scholastic realm. Ah, yes, the last time he'd been over to tune the piano, about a year ago, he had seen a table piled high with annotated papers.

"That's all couples ever seem to talk about once the wooing is done." Fulham laughed heartily, munching on a piece of peanut brittle, sending sticky brown shards down his white shirt and navy suspenders.

Augustus nodded and bid them farewell.

Yes. That seemed to be true.

His heart gave a bitter thump, so hard as to be noticeable. Surely, it should not be that way? Life was so long and varied. Surely love wasn't supposed to fade to mere household chores and children's needs? God made Eve from Adam's rib so she would be at his side, not under him. Otherwise, wouldn't the Lord have made her from Adam's sole?

Augustus recalled broaching this topic with Reverend Chambers once. It hadn't gone terribly well.

Even if a man and woman are nothing alike, then they must share new interests together or be feverishly interested in hearing what the other does.

Again, though his mind pointed out that he had no call to insert his opinions into Miss Mumford's life, he couldn't help but think that she deserved someone who was interested in her as a person, not simply a "wife."

This is why I'm still a bachelor.

Back to the jelly eggs. Or beans, depending on whether you listened to his father or to him.

Chapter Seven

"There you are, you stubborn devil. Come here. Look what I've got."

A juicy piece of whitefish was pulled through the grass, tied to a bit of string.

"You'll never grab him that way."

The large black cat sat and stared at the two men at the bottom of the hill. It was motionless except for the tiny twitch of its tail tip.

"You'll see. No cat can resist fresh fish."

"That one seems to resist just fine."

"I'm ruining my trousers for this."

"Your mother will soak 'em in something, Horace."

"She'll have to. But in a few months' time, Rowena Mumford'll be in charge of my trousers. Everything to do with my trousers." There was a leer on the young face with its large lips and too-round eyes. The fishmonger's assistant had an unfortunate resemblance to some of his wares.

"Horace Canby!"

"Oh, shut up, Parks. I'm speaking practically."

His companion, the grocer's assistant, huffed silently, eyes to the blue sky above. "I doubt that. Isn't she a bit old for you? You ought to leave this to the older men in town, like Mr. Ruger and Mr. Raine."

"If you weren't courting Clara, you wouldn't say that. Oh, this is getting us nowhere. I have to be back at the shop by two. I'm going to make a grab for him." Horace crouched, balanced on the balls of his feet, ready to chase down the black cat as it sat staring at him. But just as he lifted his haunches to run, the cat took off like a black streak of lightning.

Parks rose and grasped his friend's shoulder. "That's uncanny. I think it understands us."

"Don't talk nonsense, Parks!" exclaimed Horace, though he was shaken by the cat's abrupt departure. "I-it must have heard the bell in my trouser pocket, that's all."

"They do say that Rowena Mumford's mother's people lived here for a long time. Back in the days of the witch trials."

"Half the people in Cedar Point lived in Massachusetts during the trials. It's all nonsense. There are no such things as witches."

Parks watched a black streak across the spring grass and shivered. "I'd not marry her. Not even if she were the only woman in town, Horace. Sometimes I bring her groceries in the winter, and sometimes she comes down to the shop to get them herself. She doesn't behave like other women."

****

Rowena was met by an agitated Tiger pacing in the parlor. "I'm sorry. This plan is definitely hard on you. But, look at it this way, if you help me find a suitable fellow, I'll be happy. You'll be happy. And if...if by some miracle"—Rowena paused in front of the portrait of her parents—"I ever get married, you'll have to live with him, too. Now stop sulking. I'll give you your own bowl of chowder. Heaven only knows you're the reason I have vats of the stuff. I might see if I can press Mr. Warwick to take some home when he comes to tune the piano."

"Mrrrr." Tiger rubbed himself against his mistress' ankles as she parted the heavy drapes to let in the sunshine.

"I just have time to set yours out, but I don't have time to heat it on the stove," Rowena hissed, no longer nonchalant. She only had a few moments before Mr. Warwick arrived. She had to make sure she looked presentable after her hectic errand.

****

Augustus rode a bicycle he'd modified himself. It had a large wooden cart behind it, held with an axle and chains, with slats fitted to a special backboard he'd made. The cart was painted green with gilt letters which proclaimed, "Warwick's Whimsies, Main Street. Warwick's Bicycle and Instrument Repair, Turnbridge Alley." "Augustus Warwick, Proprietor" was painted in smaller letters underneath. It was folly to think that he needed a sign. Any other tradesman had a cart or wagon pulled by a horse, and a few used automobiles. His bicycle-cart was well-known in Cedar Point.

The last push up the hill, past the trolley line, was the hardest, especially with the weight of his tools in the back. As he sweated and strained, Augustus' mind was also struggling.

Should I tell her that this silly scheme with the cat is no way to find a suitable man?

Should I tell her I know what it's like living in this town and not quite measuring up to the part you're meant to play?

Another thought assailed him as he reached the peak of the hill and saw Rowena Mumford out on her patio, probably waiting for him. When she spotted him, she beamed and waved.

He almost lost control of his machine. *Should I try to catch that cat myself?*

All of their lives in the same town, and Augustus Warwick realized he'd never really looked at Rowena Mumford before.

He was quite the fool.

****

"Thank you for coming, Mr. Warwick." Rowena's smile was twofold. She was pleased that her piano would be tuned before the spring recital she always held for her pupils, and she loved that out of all the eligible men in Cedar Point, Augustus Warwick had never treated her as anything more than a customer.

"It's my pleasure, Miss Mumford." The tall man with broad shoulders stuck out his hand and shook hers, working her arm like the handle of a stubborn pump. Then, he winced, a tiny wince that most people wouldn't have noticed.

Rowena was not most people. She overlooked the fact that he'd shaken her hand heartily, like a man would grasp a man's hand, not as most men delicately clasped feminine fingers for a fleeting moment. "Don't stand on ceremony. Come in! Would you like some chowder when you're done?"

"I…Certainly. Yes."

"And if you have room in your cart to take some home, perhaps to your parents, you must let me send you with a few quart jars."

Augustus tugged on his flat, heather gray cap in a show of thanks. "That would be very welcome. Into the parlor?"

"Yes, go right ahead. I'll be in the kitchen."

"Oh. If you have work to do…" Augustus pointed to the large desk spread with papers.

Rowena hesitated. She never discussed her written work. But there was something in the way Mr. Warwick acted that made her curious. "Do you…do you think it appropriate for a woman to work, Mr. Warwick?"

"I don't see why not. Provided she has time in the day for all she needs to do." He set out a heavy leather satchel by the piano. It clinked and clanked.

"What about…a married woman?"

He paused as he lifted the lid of the piano. "That's a matter for the wife and her husband. Seems to me, women have always worked. Raising a family and keeping a home running is no small task. Aside from that—" He bent his head over the piano and began plucking the strings inside its long wooden body. "—don't half of the women in town work at the family business? Mrs. Chambers is fully half of the church work. Reverend Chambers fills the pulpit, and she fills the pews."

She couldn't help it. Rowena burst out laughing. "I'll go get that chowder warming."

****

Augustus lost himself in his work. There was a delicacy in tuning that most people couldn't understand, a perfect stillness as you waited for chords and tones to swell and ring together, perfectly matched. He was so focused on a stubborn lower G that was just a hair off that he didn't notice the giant black cat that had crawled into his workbag until he went to reach for a different tuning fork.

"Oh! Hello there. That can't be a comfortable place to sit, can it?" Augustus stroked the cat sitting on a jumble of metal and wood, then reached underneath him. The large head butted his hand, looking for another round of petting. "All right, I have time for a quick scratch under the chin, but that's about it. Your mistress isn't paying me to tickle her cat." Augustus tried to keep his voice stern, but it was no good. He'd always had a soft spot for animals. One thing he had always hated as a boy was seeing the tired horses drooping in their harnesses at the end of the day. He was thrilled when bicycles became more common, and he was sure automobiles would be the next big thing.

"Here now, get out of that. You wouldn't like it anyway." Augustus gently prodded the fluffy black fur to urge the cat out of his bag. The cat obeyed but took a little drawstring pouch away with him.

"Those are not treats for cats. They taste of licorice, not fish." Augustus crawled from under the piano as Tiger dragged away a pouch he'd absentmindedly tossed in with his tools. "Fine, fine, you can have the string!"

****

Rowena poked her head in to see the spectacle of the man, by all accounts quite a solitary individual, nattering away to her cat and swiping a bag back from him. However, he did pull the string out of the bag and toss it to the cat.

Tiger regarded the string for a minute, nibbled it, and then went back to the bag, pawing it until it fell on the carpet, dumping half of its contents on the floor when Warwick was back to his work, muscular shoulders visible under a thin white shirt.

Rowena hastily returned her attention to the cat. "I'm sorry. Is Tiger bothering you?" She hurried in and scooped up the bag, placing it firmly on her desk.

"Not at all. He just wants to play with the bits of string on the bag." Augustus flashed her a smile over his shoulder.

Those very...attractive shoulders. With that tousle of coppery auburn curls.

Rowena shook herself.

"He's always underfoot." She tsked, swooping down to collect the hefty feline in both arms.

"He's doing no harm," Augustus said quickly. "I'm a guest in his home, not the other way around." He went back to work, whistling the pitch of each note he plucked, letting the mellow sound of the tuning fork merge before moving up the octave.

Rowena hustled Tiger away, checking his neck. Augustus Warwick owned a bicycle repair shop. He must have had a bell somewhere about him. He had actually had his hand on the cat.

"He didn't try to slip anything on you, did he? Maybe he thinks it's too bold. Or perhaps he hasn't heard," she whispered to Tiger as she put him down in front of a bowl of creamy chowder and shut the kitchen room door to keep him inside. Not that she *wanted* Augustus Warwick to pay court to her. Still, it was time to get a cat's eye view of the situation...

Chapter Eight

Rowena did not know much about her strange affliction. Her parents were the only two who knew of her secret, and they'd taken it to the grave. Now, she bore her trouble alone.

Not that Rowena found it troubling, personally, but she knew others most assuredly would. The story went that a short time after her parents were wed, they had become much moved by a visiting missionary who worked abroad in the out-of-the-way corners of Asia and Africa. They decided that God had blessed them with enough wealth, good health, and young, strong bodies, so that they ought to do something with them before children came along. Thus, they went into the mission field, going places few others dared to go.

Her father always told the story, for it upset her mother too much to talk at length about what had happened. They had become local fixtures in a tiny town surrounded by farms. The people who came to their tent church were mostly farmers and craftsmen. Perhaps it was her father's charm or her mother's gentleness that had won them friends. Perhaps it was because her parents were adventurous, trying the local foods and customs, working the land, and doing whatever was asked of them. Whatever the reason, they were beloved by most.

"It was no act of ill will, Rowena"—her father would intone—"when the farmer's house caught fire. It was the dry season, and a fierce wind was blowing. The house went up like kindling, but your mother rushed back inside, determined to save the farm cat. A giant of a cat, big and black, almost invisible in the smoke, and the best ratter you could ask for. No birds or vermin dared come near that farm, thanks to him. The farmer had named him Rex. King, you know. He looked like a cat fit for an empress, black as night, long silky fur...I think he was part panther! Your mother saved the life of the king of the cats, that I'm sure of."

Rowena would laugh, rocking on his knee, looking at her blushing mother. This was a fairy story, surely, one of her father's clever tales to make her tired before bedtime.

But then, each time he told it, he added more. When she was about eight, he got to the part about the voyage home.

"After the farmer's house was rebuilt and the rainy season came, your mother and I set sail for home. I couldn't leave my partners in the firm indefinitely." Her father had stopped rocking her, reaching his hand out to seize his wife's hand, giving her a tender look. "Your mother was always a good sailor. This time she wasn't. I thought perhaps it was the rough sea. Then, I thought, perhaps it was a sign that you were on the way, poppet."

"Mayhew!" her mother would unfailingly gasp.

"But it wasn't that, Rowena," he went on. "It was some fever that festered and wouldn't leave. I thought I was about to lose her. Her beautiful black hair was falling out." Here her father's hand twirled a tendril of her mother's hair around his finger, while his other hand rested atop her head. They were an exact match, the locks on her mother's head and the locks on her own.

A voice that trembled with emotion continued the tale. "Her cheeks were so pale, and her eyes were so sunken. We were still a week away from England. There was no doctor on board this little transport vessel. One night, your dear mother's breathing became so labored that I thought I was losing my dear wife, and that I'd not see her again until I joined her on the other side of Jordan…" Rowena was squeezed between her parents like jam between bread, jostling to stay on her father's lap while her arms were flung around her mother's neck.

"This is the part you must keep secret, poppet. Can you promise me on all that is holy?" She always nodded. "I saw her transform. From a sickly woman in a bed to a sleeping black cat, the spitting image of the one your mother had saved. I tell you, I thought I had the fever as well. I thought I was hallucinating and going mad. I did the only thing I could think of, which was to call for the nearest member of the crew to tell me what he saw. And true as the Good Book, he said he saw a black cat curled up in my bed! Then he told me he wanted money so as not to tell the captain. When I told him that that was my wife and she had saved a cat from a fire at our last outpost, he nodded and put his hand back in his pocket. 'Ah. Cats have nine lives, Mr. Mumford. He gave your wife one of his because she saved the other eight. Your wife will get well now!' "

"And Mama did," Rowena always chimed.

"Yes, darling. I did. In a very little while, we had you. This is the part you mustn't tell, Rowena. After I had you…I never transformed again. I believe I passed my gift onto you. You must need it more."

"But why can't I tell?" Rowena hadn't understood. This was a silly game. She had never turned into a cat!

No one could do that.

"People might not believe it was a gift, a miracle. We know, serving in the wilds of the world, that the Lord works in mysterious ways. I don't know what you will do with your gift, but your mother made it work to her advantage. A cat can go where most people cannot. A cat can listen unnoticed. Your mother's sharp ears saved many lives before we left the mission field for good. That is all I'll say. Perhaps someday you will do the same." Her father had looked so grave, but his eyes sparkled. Rowena took that look to be one of pride.

"But…I can't…"

"I think one day you will…if you need to." Her mother had firmly ended the discussion. "It's our little secret. Come, Rowena. Dress for dinner."

****

This wasn't life or death. It wasn't needed. Rowena hoped her mother and father wouldn't be too disappointed. Slinking through the sliver of the open door, she padded down the stairs and into the parlor. Augustus was still leaning over the piano.

Rowena's paws padded over the soft carpet. Her senses enhanced, became more feline, in this form. Her black nose sniffed as her whiskers went into overdrive.

Anise?

Licorice.

Oh, divine.

Rowena started nibbling one of the little black beads on the carpet, always assuming the part of the feline with ease. Granny Nesbitt would faint if she knew her granddaughter was eating off the floor. That *might* be worse than finding out her daughter and granddaughter could shape-shift.

"How's my new friend? You only love me for my strings and nibbles, is that it?"

Rowena jumped, her mouth full, as Augustus' hand landed on her spine. He stroked her, one long, smooth swipe.

"You like the licorice eggs, do you? Ugh. That sounds horrible."

The man lay down on the floor beside her.

Rowena watched as he scooted under the piano, a bottle and rag in his hand.

"Sticky pedal action. Soon sorted." He went to work on the pedal, still chatting to the cat. "They come apart. Too soft."

The pedals? Rowena cocked her head. "Mrow?"

"Clever, like your mistress. The jelly eggs. Jelly beans, my father calls them. They go all soft. They need some sort of coating to keep them chewy on the outside and soft in the middle. A bit of chemistry will be involved."

He looked over at her, although of course, he believed he was merely watching a cat. His handsome face (how had she never noticed that Augustus Warwick was shockingly handsome, with that wide jaw and laughing eyes?) was wreathed in smiles. Nothing about him spoke of arrogance.

Simply himself.

"Most people think I sit on my backside all day, eating sweets. They don't know how much scientific process there is to candy-making. And any man who thinks his wife does nothing but cook and clean…by thunder, let him try it! Only doing the cooking would exhaust half of them."

Rowena couldn't help herself. She purred and

nodded.

"You seem quite human, Tiger."

She froze, eyes wide.

"You know just what I'm saying, don't you? That's why you get into such trouble about town. You think you're human." He reached out and chucked her under the chin with one crooked finger. "You're just doing your shopping. Bit of cod here. Bit of milk there. And licorice sweets, apparently. I'll give you one when we see each other next. You pop into the shop anytime you fancy. I'll let you sleep on all the tools you could want." He laughed and finished with the pedal, rising to test it. His fingers played a soft melody that he sustained with the brassy pedal, letting it ring and fill the room. "Ahh. I hope Miss Mumford thinks it's satisfactory."

Rowena hesitated. That was her cue. She had to appear before he went into the kitchen and let Tiger out, or went calling through the house for her. Either action could result in her secret being discovered.

Glad that cats had no social compunctions, she darted from the room and back up the stairs.

As soon as she was inside her bedroom, she transformed, body flowing and writhing, twisting from coal black to milky white, the fur sliding inward and upward until it was one with her ebony hair. Into a dress, with nothing underneath. Mr. Warwick wouldn't notice.

She swallowed hard.

Such thoughts…

****

"Thank you so much, Mr. Warwick. It plays like a dream, and the pedal is as smooth as silk." Rowena ran her hands over the keys and let the opening of a Bach cantata shimmer in the air, resounding in the sunny parlor.

Augustus stared at her. With her hair hanging free and the sun hitting her, she seemed to glow. Heavenly music. Heavenly beauty.

But the woman seemed all too close to earth and earthly desires. With a cough, he forced himself to make the appropriate replies, stumbling to compliment her playing and remind her to book next year's tuning.

"Oh, your jelly…blobs." Rowena seized the pouch from the lip of the piano.

"They are blobs, aren't they?" He laughed ruefully. "I'd better get my formula right. As I was telling your cat—oh." Why had the Lord suddenly made him chatty? Where was his father's taciturn bearing when it could be useful?

"Go on," Rowena murmured, stepping closer.

He tried. Honestly. It wasn't his fault that she suddenly seemed so…soft. The age of fitted dresses, long sleeves, high collars, corsets, and wide hats made women look so…pinched. Stiff. Unapproachable. At least, to a man like him. Right now, all he wondered was why Rowena Mumford looked like she belonged in his arms.

"My cat?" she prodded.

"I was talking aloud. To the cat." He sounded like a lunatic.

She smiled at him. "Tiger is an excellent listener. He rarely interrupts." She winked.

His heart buzzed in an unfamiliar way. "Yes! Well, I was telling the big fellow that these jelly eggs aren't quite working out. They need something to set them, but let them stay soft and chewy on the outside. No hard sugar candy, and no gooey boiled sweets, for fear the little darlings will rip their teeth out."

"A puzzlement, indeed. One of my contacts from Oberlin—" Rowena froze mid-sentence.

"Yes?"

"A chemist."

Augustus tilted his head, hair flopping into his eyes. *Wonderful. The most beautiful woman in town, and I stand before her like a sheepdog in need of a trim.* "What about her?"

The soft look was gone, replaced by a stiffness in her spine, her blue dress pulling tight to her shoulders as she forced them back. "Her?"

"I beg your pardon. Of course, you surely could have met a friend of the male persuasion."

"You assumed the chemist was a woman."

What had he done wrong?

He was sure his father would have a very long list. "I'm sorry?" he hazarded.

Her stiffness vanished. "Oh, Mr. Warwick, no need to apologize. I'm sorry. I'm delighted that you did not assume that only a man possessed the brains necessary to become a chemist. She works in Paris. They are experimenting with an edible starch mold that coats medicinal liquids. I believe it is a simple formula. I could wire her for it. Provided you credit her with the formula should the jelly birds take off."

"Beans."

"Beans?"

"Not birds. And not eggs, apparently. Jelly beans it is. My father wins. He often does." Augustus gave a rueful sigh as he closed his bag and took a step toward the door.

Squish.

"Oh."

"That naughty cat." Rowena clucked her tongue, blushing. "I'm so sorry about your shoe."

"And I about your carpet. Let me see if I can—" He bent.

She stooped.

Heads collided.

Through the pain, Augustus marveled that even her forehead was soft as it bashed his nose.

"Are you all right, Miss Mumford?" he demanded, taking her arm and helping her sit on the piano stool.

"Your nose is bleeding, Mr. Warwick."

There was absolutely no reason that they should laugh, and yet that's exactly what they did.

Chapter Nine

"Miss Mumford. How are you this lovely evening?" Professor Trilby swept off the trolley and trotted up the hill.

For once, Rowena didn't watch for the nightly suitors with the usual amount of dread. In fact, she smiled, remembering how Mr. Warwick had joined her for an impromptu lunch of chowder and homemade oyster crackers after his nose had stopped bleeding. Tiger had slept between their feet, occasionally nibbling at a loose thread from Mr. Warwick's trouser cuff. "It's been a busy day, Professor, but pleasant. How were your seminars?"

"Agreeable, Miss Mumford, very agreeable." He bowed low as he stood beside her porch railing, his light-gray suit jacket tinkling as he did so. "We never made arrangements the other day. That was a most unfortunate business with the milkman."

"Arrangements?" Her dark eyebrows rose in beautiful arches, naturally dark pink lips forming a puzzled but polite smile.

"To attend the readings, my dear Miss Mumford. I shall be giving a reading of Mr. John Greenleaf Whittier. Perhaps you'd favor us with something from the Scriptures?"

"Perhaps. What night is—"

"Miss Mumford, what a beautiful night. Good

evening, Professor." Mr. Ruger strode up, his wide frame dwarfing Trilby's with companionable ease. "Miss Mumford, the candy shop is open late. Please, come with me and offer your opinion on some sweets for the Osterhasen baskets."

As Mr. Ruger stepped closer, she heard another melodic sound. She hid her knowing smile by turning away to pluck a dead leaf off of an impatient plant. Two of her eligible suitors seemed to be rising to the challenge. Unless she was much mistaken, both of them had concealed bells upon their person. But what really prompted her to say yes to Mr. Ruger was not the fact that both men were interested in her challenge. Her heart did a quick thump, a quite *unexpected* thump, when she thought about seeing Augustus again.

"Let me just get my hat and gloves, Mr. Ruger. Professor Trilby, I certainly would love to attend your literary evening. Did you call upon Miss Earnshaw and invite her as well?"

"Well, no. Not as yet," the tall, thin professor stammered.

"Oh, but you simply must! She is ever so fond of your work." Rowena knew this was a slight exaggeration, but she pressed on, nodding with her blue eyes wide. "She heard you speak on the sacred carols at Christmas, Professor. She was much moved and is eager to hear you read again. If only your seminary admitted young ladies..." Rowena trailed off, eyes now averted. She'd led him to a promising place where he could easily win favor.

Or lose it swiftly. "I can see no use for a woman in a theological college, Miss Mumford." Trilby looked torn between waging an argument and pleased at her praise.

"You cannot see the value of a woman studying the Scriptures for her own edification? Or to help her father and mother, or perhaps her husband, in the mission field?" Her voice took on a distinctly chilly air, and Trilby deflated.

"In that case, I would dearly love to discuss such matters with the fairer sex, if you'll pardon the expression, Miss Mumford. I will call upon the Earnshaws and ask if Miss Earnshaw would like to accompany us. That does seem more appropriate. I'll be pleased to escort you *both*." With that parting shot across Mr. Ruger's bow, Trilby bowed so low that he had to make a frantic swipe in midair to catch his falling glasses. Glasses secured, he turned on his heel and marched away.

"I'll fetch my purse, gloves, and hat," Rowena said to Mr. Ruger, who was frowning after Trilby's departing back.

"And perhaps a wrap," Mr. Ruger suggested. "It is still a bit chilly on these April evenings. Perhaps we might stroll around the pond afterward and sample what we purchase?"

Her face twisted into a small smile that she hoped was not too bitter. She'd never cared much for sugary things, and since her parents' passing…Her appetite was a function of existence rather than pleasure. "Oh Mr. Ruger, I do not have much taste for sweets. You needn't buy—"

"It is for the children," Mr. Ruger said sternly, but there was a twinkle in his eye.

"Well." Rowena had to smile at the memory of her hastily consumed licorice drop from earlier. "I do have a soft spot for one or two things. Make yourself comfortable." Rowena gestured to the wicker glider on the porch. "I won't be a moment."

****

Rowena slipped indoors, leaving the door carefully ajar. She bit her lip once she was certain that Mr. Ruger was facing the quiet tree-lined avenue again. Yes, she could see him out there rocking on the glider, his straw boater on his knee, looking like the king of the castle. She also saw Matthew Raine approaching with an abundance of early tulips in a bright yellow ribbon.

How thoughtful.

And what better way to test my plan and kill two birds with one stone?

****

"I say, Wolfgang, what are you doing? Waiting until the lady arrives home?" Matthew Raine nimbly hopped up the porch steps as if he owned the place. He leaned on one of the porch's white wooden pillars, draping his arm around it as if he were an ivy vine, the yellow and pink tulips flung across his bent knee.

"No, Matthew, tonight is my night. Rowena and I are heading to Warwick's. Then perhaps we'll take a walk around the pond in the park."

"The girl is a fool. She'd rather hang out with a mustachioed German sausage like you than a man who won't sandpaper her nose when he kisses her?" Raine sneered.

"My whiskers prove that I'm a full-blooded man, Raine. What do your smooth cheeks say about you?" Ruger countered, face ruddy with indignation.

"Whatever my cheeks may say, I'm sure they can bring a blush to a few maiden ones," Matthew boasted, his voice low and the insinuation obvious.

Rowena had heard enough. Her clothes were piled under a shawl in the hall coat closet, and Tiger was sleeping in the kitchen with the door shut.

Saying a prayer that this would not be her undoing, Rowena allowed herself to shrink, her long black hair enveloping her naked frame until she strode out onto the patio, padding on four delicate paws, sleek and silky. She looked at the world from shin-height through bright blue eyes in a furry black face.

Breath clenched in her low-slung rib cage, Rowena paused, the pink pads of her paws flexing on the whitewashed boards of the porch.

"There's the precious pet now," muttered Matthew.

"Oh, he's bigger than I thought." Ruger shrunk back a bit.

"What's the matter? I thought you were such a prime specimen of manhood!" Raine mocked. "Don't tell me that a little cat spooks you?"

"*Nein, nein,*" Ruger protested, hand going to his pocket. "I'm not afraid of any of God's creatures. Only, one does hear stories about *that* cat. Didn't he once bite the fishmonger?"

"More like a playful nip." Matthew chuckled. "Mind you, after that, he hired young Horace Canby to do his deliveries."

Rowena stretched and arched her back, quite liking the uninhibited feeling that came with her feline form. She turned her slinking frame to Mr. Ruger.

Matthew sprang out and pounced on Ruger's shoulders, shaking him with both hands.

The larger man jumped and let out a few harsh guttural words that Rowena didn't understand.

His assailant only laughed, wagging his finger in the bewhiskered face. "Careful, Ruger, a tailor without all of his fingers isn't much of a tailor, is he?"

As Ruger sank back, glaring at the smirking dandy, Matthew reached into his pocket and pulled out a string with a bell on it.

"Already done up in a knot." Matthew slowly eased into a crouch. "A quick slip over its head…"

"Matthew, she'll be back in a moment!" Ruger hissed.

"Which is why I'm going to win this contest and the fair Miss Mumford, Wolfie." Matthew tensed, the string stretched over his spread fingers, bell tinkling as it swayed.

"This was *my* evening with her, Matthew."

"You've got your own bell, you coward. No one is stopping you from putting it on the blasted creature."

Rowena froze as the two men crept toward her, one with slow, predatory movements, and the other with cautious, lingering steps. Ruger had been goaded into action, but he was acting all the same.

With a sudden lunge, Matthew Raine grabbed her by the back of the neck, hard enough to seal her throat and make her eyes bulge. The foolish man hadn't realized that he couldn't possibly fit the collar over her head while he was dangling her in the air with his fist.

Claws unsheathed and tail lashing, Rowena dug her back feet into his arm and twisted free as he dropped her. Ruger dove at her as she scampered back into the house.

Breathing hard and blinking back tears, Rowena transformed in the safety of the kitchen, struggling into her dress and hat while bruises formed on her milky skin.

"Never in a million years. Neither of them," she

vowed, hands shaking. She nearly stabbed herself as she fastened a broach at her throat, the high collar of her dress serving a dual purpose. It would hide the bruises and fend off the night's chill.

She was still going with Mr. Ruger into town.

Rowena told herself it was because he had been the more reticent, the more kindly of the two.

But in reality, she knew she wanted to be near Augustus Warwick, the man who treated women like equals and animals like people.

Chapter Ten

Augustus whistled as he rinsed the shaving lather off of his face. He gave the mirror a glowing smile.

The world was a wonderful place. Spring was a glorious season.

And his father was right.

Well, everything couldn't be completely perfect, not in this sinful world.

Rowena had called to his shop with Wolfgang Ruger two nights ago, but the woman couldn't have made it any plainer that they were there on a joint mission, not on an outing as a courting couple. She barely spoke to her escort, instead addressing the majority of her questions to him.

The more they talked, the easier it became. She laughed. He laughed. Wolfie laughed. Samples went flowing out as Rowena applied her pencil and Ruger applied his knowledge of Osterhasen traditions.

"Like having friends," Augustus told the shiny copper kettle as he stared at his reflection. It was time for a batch of chocolate walnut fudge.

Rowena liked chocolate walnut fudge.

Rowena liked licorice drops.

She liked blackberry phosphates, lime cordials, and roasted Virginia peanuts, and...*him.*

Yes, he believed it was true, especially after she came back the next morning, alone, forest-green skirts shimmering in the sun as she strode up Main Street. He wasn't working in the sweet shop, but repairing the grocer's bicycle in the rear. Miss Mumford had ventured into the alley and found him, pulling a folded telegram from her dainty silk purse, standing as easily among the detritus of broken wheels and gears as she had among bonbons and polished glass.

And then...oh, miracle. She had asked how he would make the molds and then watched him fetch his tin snips and start a fire in the iron barrel he kept for metalworking. She had stayed and talked about her time at Oberlin and her friend the chemist while he'd cobbled together a long strip of tin, indenting it with the handle of a pair of pliers until there were a hundred little oval grooves in it.

"When that cools, I'll attempt the liquid capsule method and pour in a batch of my strawberry jellies," he had said, sweating and sooty.

"You're so clever with your hands and your tools, Mr. Warwick." Rowena Mumford had smiled at him, standing by his elbow, close enough for her skin to take on a rosy glow from the dying fire in the barrel.

He had felt hot all over, and it had nothing to do with the flames.

****

Now, Augustus stood humming over his counter, ready to test the maiden batch. Lining a tray with a long piece of cheesecloth, he flipped the mold over and...out came a hundred little pink ovals, rolling merrily, not splodging out in unset blobs.

"I did it!" he shouted in the empty shop. "Well, to be fair, *we* did it, Miss Mumford, her chemist friend, and I." Even when there was no one to hear him, he gave credit where credit was due. He'd have to go make a few more of these trays and another batch of the liquid that filled them, and then dozens of batches of his fruity concoction to fill the molds. He had thousands to make if he wanted each child to have a bright, full bag of these jelly beans.

As quickly as triumph and joy entered his soul, they ebbed away at the daunting prospect. Not that he was afraid of hard work—Augustus had just realized that extra hours in his candy kitchen would leave less chances for him to see Miss Mumford.

"Which is very silly, as I only see her a few times a year outside of church functions. I see her to tune her piano and when she comes in to buy a box of peppermint sticks for her grandmother's birthday." He had never before realized how little he saw her, and how much more he would *like* to see her. His troubled thoughts also brought up the fact that there were others with far better chances of courting the lady effectively, having both time and means.

With a mournful sigh at his own foolishness, Augustus tipped the fudge into trays to cool. *Half the men in Cedar Point must be paying court to Rowena Mumford, and I just committed myself to two weeks of making tiny rainbow jelly eggs. Beans.*

Does it matter what they're called? They'll make the children happy. They'll make the ladies of the church happy.

So why do I feel so…morose?

Deciding that he might as well be profitable while trapped in his sweet shop, Augustus went to the front of the door and switched the wooden sign with its curlicues of gilt paint from "Closed" to "Open." As he opened the door to let the scent of fudge waft into the street and lure in customers, he saw that someone was already waiting for admittance.

"It's Tiger, isn't it?" Augustus bent down and looked at the giant, shaggy black cat. Its fur certainly seemed worse for wear than the last time he had seen it. The cat was covered in dust and bits of potato peel.

"Are you out on your morning errands as well? Well, you needn't go crawling through my rubbish bins. I know just what you'd like." Augustus hurried to the barrels of sweets and grabbed a few licorice drops in his hand.

When he turned back, he found the feline had taken up residence in the middle of the floor, sunning itself in the golden rectangle made by the open door.

"I remember you like your licorice. You're a strange cat, aren't you? Hm? Not today?" Augustus watched Tiger bat the candies away, then tuck his paw over his head. "I don't know if you'll be good for business, lying there like that. If you're going to visit Warwick's Whimsies, you'll have to be a bit more presentable. Now, if you'd slunk round the back and into the repair shop…"

The cat blinked sleepy green eyes at him. Augustus sighed. "Well, hold still." He shook a spare tea towel from the pocket of his apron. Crouching beside the sunning visitor, he wiped him down. "There. You don't look perfect, but at least you're not wearing scraps."

"Good morning, Mr. Warwick."

Augustus sprang up so fast he almost lost his balance. His hair flopped, and his cheeks flamed.

It was Carrie Earnshaw, the daughter of the dour, imminently respectable Captain Earnshaw, a man known for his love of a tight ship, even on dry land. If she told her father that Augustus Warwick was kneeling in the middle of his shop, wiping potato peelings off a cat—he'd never live it down. What's more, Captain Earnshaw and Colonel Warwick had become the best of friends after the colonel's retirement from the army.

When his father heard…

"Can I help you, Miss Earnshaw?" Augustus finally found his voice.

"I-is that Miss Mumford's cat?" the girl stammered, her pale, pinched face squinting against the sun as she hovered outside of the shop.

"It is. He wandered in."

"Wh-what were you doing to him?"

"Getting the potato peelings off of him." Augustus winced, not from the sun in his eyes, but from the absurdity of his answer. "I think he'd been exploring the remains of someone's dinner."

"That sounds like Tiger."

"He has quite a reputation."

"He does." Miss Earnshaw nodded, clutching her white knitted wrap more tightly around her shoulders.

Augustus thought she looked nervous, as if she were waiting for something bad to happen. Unbidden, rumors of Tiger's transgressions with various townsfolk came to mind. "He likes me, I think. I doubt he'll bite. From what I've heard, there's always a reason when animals lash out."

"He bit the fishmonger once."

"And if I know the fishmonger, I imagine a broom handle was involved." Augustus crossed his arms. "If the fish were where the cat could get at it, it wasn't fresh nor fit to be sold. And why batter a dumb creature over something that would have gone into the fertilizer heap, anyway?"

Far from nervous now, the young woman's eyes shone, and her smile filled her entire face. "I agree, Mr. Warwick. Please, could you help me choose a gift for Miss Mumford?"

It was his turn to look flustered, blinking and completely faithless to his code of service and salesmanship, he exclaimed, "Why? Miss Mumford? Me? Why?"

Carrie laughed and walked in, stepping carefully past the dozing miniature panther. "The evening post brought wonderful news, Mr. Warwick. I have been invited to sit the entrance examination for Radcliffe. In no small part, that's thanks to Miss Mumford."

"Congratulations!" Augustus lost his sense of propriety yet again and shook her hand as he would a man's, pumping the thin, delicate arm until the young lady's hat was askew and her shawl had fallen off one shoulder. "Indeed, cause for celebration. A strawberry soda, courtesy of Warwick's Whimsies."

She took a seat, tittering, her cheeks pink. Augustus thought that when she smiled, her face transformed.

"You are too kind, Mr. Warwick. Not even my own brothers made such a fuss."

"Perhaps they are still in shock. I like to see women getting an education, doing what they dream of. My mother—" Silence replaced his jovial air. Augustus turned his back to the counter and started chipping ice into a tall glass.

"Your mother? Was she a conservatory woman? Or even a college graduate?"

"No. Nothing like that."

His mother was the wife of an officer, first,

foremost, and always. When his father traveled, he left her alone raising two children with no family nearby. When the gallant colonel asked if his wife minded staying behind, her answer was always no. When his father left, Augustus would hear her crying late into the night, would see her spending days at the window, writing feverish letters, and sewing and knitting endless socks and scarves.

His father's letters were few and brief.

His father's career was idyllic, a dream, full of medals, bravery, and a steady climb up the ranks.

His mother's dream?

She never spoke of it, but Augustus knew it.

All she wanted was to be by her husband's side. She never even considered doing something for herself or telling her husband that he was unwittingly breaking her heart.

Once, Augustus had asked her why she looked so sad. She'd smiled through her tears and said, "That's how it is for women, my darling boy."

That didn't seem right to Augustus. Not for women nor for their husbands.

"I'm proud of your success, Miss Earnshaw. Proud of Miss Mumford's as well," Augustus finally said, placing the drink in front of her with a fixed smile and downcast eyes. "I'm not sure this is the best place to get Miss Mumford a gift. Perhaps a bookshop? Some new sheet music? I have a recent catalog from Boston Music Company. They have a good variety of classical pieces and—"

"She likes ragtime," Carrie blurted, shaking her head. She quickly pressed a hand to her mouth. "I'm sorry, that's a secret. Some mothers wouldn't send their children to Miss Mumford if they knew she liked that sort of music."

Augustus' brows drew together. "Then they must be fools. To name but one example, Mr. Joplin was a brilliant composer. The color of his skin and the speed of his music can't change that fact."

"Do you play? I mean, I knew you played enough to repair instruments. I've never heard you play, Mr. Warwick."

Augustus smiled and set a sliced strawberry on the edge of her glass. He knew she was referring to the church functions where anyone with even the slightest musical talent was encouraged to play and sing. Hymns, patriotic pieces, and classical offerings were the order of the day for those events. While Augustus quite enjoyed the stirring notes of "The Battle Hymn of the Republic," he wasn't proficient at playing it.

Dropping his voice, he leaned forward and whispered, "I can play by ear. I think Mrs. Chambers might faint if she heard me play the sort of music I prefer. The 'Maple Leaf Rag' is my favorite, Miss Earnshaw."

"That's Miss Mumford's favorite. My, you two have a lot in common. Mr. Warwick...do you have any bells in your repair shop?"

"Bells?" Augustus frowned. *Oh, no. What's she after now?* He cast a panicked look at the cat, which was purr-snoring loudly, its belly to the sun.

"I...want to get one for my brother's bicycle."

"Ah! Thank goodness."

She cast a shrewd eye over him as she put the straw to her lips. "Why such expressions of gratitude?"

Was it his imagination, or was there something coy and knowing in her tone? "I only have three left, Miss

Earnshaw. I'm glad you happened by in time to get one. There seems to be a regular run on bells this week."

"Funny."

"Isn't it?"

No one spoke for a moment.

"She doesn't have any siblings. Or parents. Miss Mumford, I mean. She has cousins and her grandmother. I believe she has an aunt and a few uncles scattered around. Her father's people live in England. The thing is…I don't think very many people buy her gifts, Mr. Warwick. When someone has money…well, perhaps people assume they can buy whatever they'd like. But a gift isn't about money, it's about affection. Care. Admiration. There are few people I admire or care for more than Miss Mumford. So, even if it's a silly little thing, I would like to buy her a box or bag of confection. She often gets books and papers sent to her in the post. But this will be something from her most devoted pupil and, dare I say, her friend."

He swallowed several times. Another one of the friendless. They hid in plain sight in Cedar Point, a town where everyone was *friendly*, but a few had missed out on finding the secret door that led from outward friendliness to bosom friendship.

At last, his rusty voice creaked to life. "She likes lime cordials. I'll wrap them for you."

****

"Carrie, how nice to see you. We don't have a lesson scheduled today, do we?" Rowena opened her door and stood back, letting Carrie in. For a moment, she thought about running and hiding the papers scattered across her desk, the legal books she had open as she prepared her notes on the contract that a contact in Cincinnati had asked R. Mumford, Esq. to look over.

But…No. Why must I hide? Well, I must hide some things from some people. A stab of loneliness pierced her heart. *One thing from all people.* But the fact that she consulted on legal and business matters? No, Carrie could be trusted with that secret. That secret might be inconvenient if it ever came out, but it wouldn't be deadly.

"For you, Miss Mumford. I mean, Rowena." Carrie leaned forward and pressed a pink-and-white box into her teacher's hand. "Father received a letter. I sit my entrance examination to Radcliffe on the second of May! French, English, literature, mathematics, and the sciences. Oh, I think I might faint, but it'll be from pure joy. I couldn't have done it without you."

"You most certainly could have. I merely helped." Rowena pressed the girl's cheek with her own. "Oh. These are from Warwick's."

"Lime cordials. He said you liked them."

"Well, Mr. Warwick is correct. Though how he knew…"

"I believe he is an intelligent and observant man." Carrie hovered in the foyer.

"Come and sit. Tell me all the good news." Rowena beckoned her to come into the dining room. "I'll put on a pot of tea, and we can have a celebratory sweet." She undid the ribbon on the box and dangled it off the edge of the carved cherrywood chairs in the dining room. "Tiger! Tiger, look."

"Oh, Tiger isn't here, Miss Mumford."

Rowena laughed. "Is he out gallivanting in the garden again? Or has he gone farther afield?" she called over her shoulder as she bustled into the kitchen.

"He was in Mr. Warwick's shop."

Rowena lost her grip on the dainty china cup she was pulling from the cabinet. "Was he really?"

"Yes, and he was covered in potato peelings. Mr. Warwick was cleaning him up."

"What a...thoughtful man." Rowena leaned on the counter for a minute, unable to move beyond the act of setting two cups and saucers on a silver tray.

Tiger had been locked in the house a good deal this week. Perhaps that was why he was venturing into the heart of Main Street. He usually didn't go that far, content to cause mischief in the house or in their pretty and moderately well-to-do neighborhood at the top of the hill. To get to Main Street, the cat would have had to walk almost two-thirds of Cedar Point's trolley line.

He must be feeling cooped up.

Or he must enjoy Augustus' company.

Tiger had an uncanny ability to mirror her emotions. Even though she was alone, her cheeks turned apple bright, and her throat was hot.

"He told me in passing that he's almost sold out of bells. I imagine everyone who's bought one has been young, handsome, and unwed," Carrie ventured, pulling her simple white gloves off and laying them in her lap.

"Male, assuredly. It is still considered a bit scandalous for a woman to ride a bicycle," Rowena remarked, bringing the tray in, sans teapot. "The water will be ready in a moment." Rowena sat, the picture of distraction, unable to meet her guest's eyes, fingers fiddling with the lump sugar and the tiny cream pitcher.

"He could have a bell set aside, though. For his own use," Carrie said primly, hiding a smile.

"Carrie Earnshaw! I don't think Mr. Warwick has

the slightest interest in wooing me. If he has sold a lot of bells lately, I'm quite sure he has no idea what they're for. He seems above all the petty local gossip." Hand gently fingering the lingering bruise on the back of her neck, she sighed. She liked that about Augustus.

"Ah, but he had every chance to put a bell on Tiger, yet he didn't." Carrie's expression indicated this was a great triumph.

Her hostess couldn't figure out why. Did Carrie think she would spurn Mr. Warwick's advances? She wouldn't. In fact, his were the only ones she would care to hear, especially after witnessing the behavior of Matthew Raine, Simon Trilby, Wolfgang Ruger, and a host of others from a "cat's eye view."

"It would seem he's unaware or uninterested," Rowena said with forced cheer.

"I think he's very much aware." Carrie raised a forefinger in a gesture that reminded Rowena of Professor Trilby. She smothered a smile as the girl continued. "But he is too noble to use your beloved pet in such a fashion. He will not entrap you through Tiger. He will press his suit when all the men have had their chance to try and have failed."

"You seem to have given this a good deal of thought."

"I have." She nodded gravely. "Men know that you've set them a challenge. They will compete with each other for a chance to get to you. But Mr. Warwick seems unlike other men. He's often alone, wrapped in his own tasks. Like you." Carrie beamed and dropped three lumps of sugar into the bottom of her empty cup.

"That doesn't mean—"

"He would like to be seen for himself. Just like we

would." The smile faded. "I can tell."

Rowena swallowed a retort. Carrie probably could. Often overlooked as plain and peculiar, the girl had a keener set of ears and a sharper mind than almost anyone Rowena had ever met, even considering her years in the finest schools in Europe and the jewel of women's education, Oberlin. "My dear Carrie," Rowena murmured, giving her hand a squeeze. "What a jewel you are. You shine, my friend. Your brilliance is something you can't hide."

"Oh! I…I don't know what to say."

"Then let's leave off that subject. Tell me, did you receive any other exciting items in the post…or in person?"

"Professor Trilby asked Father if I might accompany him to a series of readings this Saturday evening. He said you'd be there."

"I shall." Rowena jumped up as she heard the kettle hissing. She couldn't help but wonder if Augustus would also like to attend…

A pity that a woman could not very well ask a man to accompany her.

****

"You know, your mistress must be getting worried about you by now. Although you've been very good for business, I admit." Augustus Warwick hung up his apron and ran his fingers through his hair. In the morning, it shone like brass, and while it was wayward, it still had a smooth glossy sheen that his mother would have been proud of. But by day's end, it invariably looked as though an angry squirrel had tried to use his hair as a nest.

Augustus had never served so many groups of

whispering men in his life. Tiger had remained stubbornly in his shop. If Augustus had been the superstitious sort who believed in witchcraft and animal familiars, he would have said that Rowena had sent the cat to town to weed out the failures among her potential suitors. To a man, they'd all proven hopeless at handling the task. As the cat had sat in the shop in full view of the street, the men walking along had stopped and pointed. Most had then wandered in, asking to try one of those delightful new ice cream cones despite that it was only ten in the morning, or asking for a penny's worth of fudge as a mere excuse. Unfailingly, one man had approached the counter while his companions set upon the sleepy black cat. Augustus didn't know exactly what they had been doing to it, but he'd heard many low growls and frantic hisses (feline), followed by yowls of pain (human). Wolfgang Ruger's shop, which was only a little ways up Main Street, had done a booming trade in handkerchiefs that day, as men had entered Warwick's Whimsies with a wink and a nudge and had left with bleeding thumbs and sweets to console themselves.

"You honestly can't stay here." Augustus nudged the cat gently with the toe of his shoe. "You were a grand success for one day, but if you stay here another, people will think that I literally charge a pound of flesh. Shoo, go on home!"

Tiger glared at him reproachfully but didn't hiss or arch his back.

"It's not that I dislike your company, old fellow—" Augustus paused, frowning. "—or young fellow, as the case may be, it's simply that I don't want to worry Miss Mumford. You are very dear to her. And I really shouldn't be standing here, chatting with a cat."

Augustus sighed. "Not that I begrudge the sales you doubtless brought me, but I barely had a moment to work on the Easter candies for the children. You mightn't know it, but Mrs. Chambers can be quite fierce when someone disappoints her." Another sigh. "It's getting dark. I don't have time to run you home in the basket of my bicycle."

Augustus paused in the doorway. Streetlamps were flickering on, but none of his usual contentment appeared. It was funny, but every argument he made when speaking to the cat only led to a greater conviction that he should do exactly what he was objecting to. He didn't have enough time to work on the jelly beans, but he would love to see Rowena Mumford. It was getting dark, and there were plenty of people about who had tried and failed to bell the cat. He didn't like the thought of Tiger being ambushed on the way home. With a sudden stomp of his foot, Augustus slapped his flat cloth cap over his head, flattening the squirrel's nest in his hair, and shrugged into his coat jacket. "Come on. I'm taking you home."

****

A strange melancholy came over Rowena after Carrie left. There was one thing that unfailingly cheered her.

She sat down at her piano bench, the shades drawn but the back garden door left open in case Tiger should come in that way. He never stayed out all night. Rowena bit her lip as she retrieved her sheet music. Should she go out and search for him now, or give him just a little longer? After all, he was quite far away, all the way down in the center of town this time.

"Mr. Joplin, I hope you can work your magic on me

tonight," she said softly as she flexed her fingers over the keys. Within moments, the sound of "Maple Leaf Rag" echoed throughout the house.

For five minutes, she was too busy smiling and lost in the skill required to worry about what the neighbors would think if they heard her playing such rollicking music, or what might have happened to her beloved pet. It was only as she was playing the last few measures that a horrifying thought struck her. What if someone had been determined to meet her challenge at any cost? What if Matthew Raine, who seemed to think that his wealth and good looks entitled him to be a bit of a bully, had captured Tiger and injured him in his struggle to put a bell on him?

Well, she would listen very politely to whatever Mr. Raine had to say if it meant getting her precious cat back. As she was searching through her piano bench for another one of Joplin's pieces to soothe her soul, a gentle tapping came from the front porch.

"Miss Mumford?" a male voice called softly.

"Thank heavens." Rowena flew to the front door, but she stopped short when she saw Augustus Warwick standing in front of it. "Mr. Warwick?" she exclaimed.

"I'm so sorry to call upon you so late, Miss Mumford," Augustus stammered and held out a large wicker basket.

"What is all this?" She was tongue-tied and fuzzy-headed from worry.

"Mrow." Tiger's head popped up from the depths of the basket, followed by the rest of him. Like a shadow, he nimbly slipped past her ankles and into the house.

"Tiger!"

"Yes, he stayed with me today. I'm sorry, I tried to

persuade him to leave." Augustus shifted the basket to one arm and twisted his hat in his free hand. "Pardon the late call. I was worried about him being out all night. Well, I was worried that *you'd* be worried." He blinked and stepped back, rocking from foot to foot. "Foolish of me. He's a fierce little chap. He seems to look after himself all right."

Rowena waved away Augustus' apology, her knees weak with relief, and her heart confused. Tiger had spent the entire day at Augustus Warwick's shop? Warwick's Whimsies was at the center of town and the place where anyone who had time to stand about sipping a frivolous drink congregated. He must have heard of her plan. Yet Tiger's neck remained bare.

Why did that cause such a stab of disappointment?

"Are you well, Miss Mumford? You look pale. I *should* have brought him home earlier. You must've been fretting for hours."

"Oh no, Mr. Warwick. Carrie Earnshaw called on me this afternoon. I knew where he was. It is *I* who should have come to fetch him. I hope he wasn't too much trouble."

With ease that Rowena envied, Augustus' tense frame relaxed. He chuckled and praised, "He was no trouble at all to me. Tiger was as good as gold, and he seemed to be a draw to the shop. I've never had so many gentlemen in my store at midday. Although whenever somebody got too close to him, Tiger didn't take kindly to it! I'm not sure if I'd have him there every day. No offense, Miss Mumford."

"Oh no," Rowena groaned, clapping her hands to her cheeks, eyes wide. "He drove off your customers?"

"I'd say he attracted them, and their own silliness

sent them away. I don't know for certain what's caused it, Miss Mumford, but it seems as though half the men in town want to be in the good graces of your cat. Per—perhaps they think that if the cat is agreeable to them, you'll also be agreeable." Augustus trailed off.

Rowena struggled to answer. When the idea had first entered her head, it had seemed wonderful...especially since she knew something that no one else did. She'd known that her secret would allow her to observe her potential suitors from a vantage point they'd never suspect.

She hadn't really thought it out fully, had she? Loneliness, grief, and anger did things to someone always on the edge of acceptability. Trying to explain that to a sensible, kind man like Mr. Warwick seemed impossible now, when the fever of inspiration had passed. Still, she'd have to try.

****

"Mr. Warwick, I confess I've had a silly—"

"What happened to your neck?" Augustus interrupted his hostess, not giving a fig for manners. Miss Mumford's simple housedress had a low collar that settled around her shoulders, and her hair was up in a loose bun. Augustus could see a spate of bruises running down the back of her lily-white neck. "You've been injured!" He squinted. The injury consisted of a large bruise on one side of her neck and four smaller ones on the other, almost as if someone had gripped her by the nape of the neck. The military spirit his father had hammered home came out in full force. Augustus drew himself up to his full height, his voice loud, his usual relaxed tones vanishing. "Did someone...has someone—"

"That is nothing, Mr. Warwick, but it is good of you to be so concerned!" Rowena laughed lightly, hastily unpinning her hair. She beamed, and Augustus succumbed, the sunshine of her smile melting his suspicions.

Augustus bit back the question he wanted to ask. *No. Mustn't pry.* "Of course. I'm sorry. I should not be here so late." He bowed himself out of the door.

Rowena followed him, biting her lower lip. It was a very unusual gesture for her, Augustus realized. Even though he'd seen her relatively few times, Miss Mumford had always appeared confident and unperturbed. Something in her manner made him hesitate at the bottom of the porch steps.

"Mr. Warwick?" She paused, one foot on the top of the whitewashed stair, one hand on the ivy-wrapped railing. "Mr. Warwick, I believe that you can tell a great deal about a person by how they treat an animal."

"I agree." His smile resurfaced.

"Yes," she continued, winding a coil of her night-sky hair around her fingertip. "I had a silly idea after being pursued by several men who don't seem to know me well, men who don't even seem to *desire* to know me well. Oh, they may desire *me*—" She paused, her face visibly pink even in the darkness. "—but as to my thoughts, feelings, and habits? No. Perhaps it is my own foolishness, as I don't give many people a chance to get to know me. There have been rumors about me because I'm an educated, independent woman."

"The rumormongers are the foolish ones." Augustus reached for her hand but quickly tucked his fingers into his trouser pocket instead.

"It is kind of you to say so, but I do grow tired of

being seen as a woman to *marry* as opposed to a woman to befriend, to know, even to be neighborly toward. But any man who would share my life would have to put up with peculiarities of mine." She smiled a tight painful grimace that didn't reach her eyes. "One of those peculiarities involves a cat."

"Oh yes, your wee panther. It is my turn for a confession, Miss Mumford. I have heard the rumors that you set the gentlemen of this town a contest. Whoever could place a bell on your cat's neck would have the right to pay a call on you and perhaps even court you. At first, when I heard the idea, I thought it was quite foolish." Augustus paused, shocked that he was revealing so much. He cursed his mother's insistence on elocution lessons. She had not wanted her son to grow up only as a rough soldier's boy with no airs and graces. Now in times of trouble, his vocabulary either deserted him or came charging in like the cavalry. He coughed off his awkwardness and concluded, "But, after seeing your plan in action all day, I think you must be even more brilliant than anyone knows. I know that bravery is to be admired and that faint heart never won fair maiden—" He studied the tips of his shoes, unable to meet her eyes. "—but there is also something to be said for gentleness and compassion. The men who tried to place a bell on Tiger's neck today went about it all wrong. They treated him like an object, just as they treat you like one. I can see he's quite the individual. He likes the sun, he likes adventure, and he's awfully fickle when it comes to his eating habits."

"Fickle?" Rowena echoed.

Augustus ignored her puzzlement. "I take back my sentiments that this was a foolish plan. I see just how well it works. A man must first pass the test of fire—or rather a test of fur." He chuckled at his own little joke.

****

Rowena laughed with him. The sound of shared laughter was a tonic, warm and soothing. She plucked up her courage. Mr. Warwick was certainly being brave, speaking so freely and admitting something that she was sure most men in Cedar Point would not—that she had a plan that surpassed his expectations and that he was wrong. He'd even admitted to having heard of the plan, giving it consideration, and amending his judgment.

Now it was her turn to be brave and to do what the women of her town would not. Looking him in the eye, she spoke softly, "I wonder why you did not try it yourself, Mr. Warwick?" She pressed her hands tight to her waist, not in a coquettish gesture, but to keep her stomach and lungs from bolting out of her mouth. She continued, "Tiger certainly seems to like you well enough."

"Oh?" Augustus cocked his head, a slight frown creasing his handsome face. "Oh, Miss Mumford, I have no illusions that I would be a suitable matrimonial candidate. I'm sure most women would like a more gentlemanly fellow with better prospects who works in a steadier industry." Augustus swallowed hard enough that Rowena could hear it and see the flexure in his neck.

"What I would like is a man who befriends me and is willing to accept that I may be a somewhat…unorthodox person as far as my habits and tastes go."

"I am quite the peculiar individual myself, at least, according to my father. I could have gone to West Point, you know," Augustus blurted.

"Why didn't you?"

"I wouldn't have been a very happy person if I had. I know happiness should not come before duty, and for that, I have disappointed my father."

"But there are all sorts of ways to fulfill the mission God gives you," Rowena whispered, her heart beating faster as she sat on the glider. She stared at him and moved to the far edge, hip pressed to the wicker arm in a silent invitation. He paused, body leaning forward before thick-soled shoes followed. Then he came up and joined her, easing in at the far end of the glider with a tip of his hat and a tiny bow.

This is how courting couples sit, Rowena thought, as they talk about everything and nothing. Talking about the future and simply being happy.

"Mr. Warwick," she said, "may I entrust you with a secret? I do not believe it would cause any breach of duty to Cedar Point or your family."

He smiled. "Indeed you may, and if you tell me a secret, I shall tell you one of mine."

She laughed. "Very well. I do not simply live off my inheritance or from teaching French and piano. I also write a business and legal column for a newspaper in Cincinnati. What's more, I have correspondence with businesses and clients who asked me to examine their contracts for legal and business suitability." She waited. She waited for him to mock or exclaim in disbelief. Instead, he shook his head, eyes wide in amazement.

"My goodness, Miss Mumford! You are a dark horse, if you'll forgive me for saying so. You have more talents than most men in this town."

"And yet you may ask yourself why didn't I become a schoolteacher or a seamstress or even a governess? The same reason you did not go to West Point, Mr. Warwick. I would not have been happy, and my parents told me that God has a purpose for me, no matter where I am or what I'm doing. My father was quite a businessman, but when he and my mother wed, they decided to spend a few years working in the mission field. They dedicated months and, as I grew older, years of their lives to serving abroad. Their last post was in India. Businessman or fisherman." She smiled, a tear in her eye. "My parents knew that they must use their talents to help others in big ways or small. You bring much joy to people through music and confection, and a mode of transportation and repairs…Oh, the list goes on." She knew she was babbling now, but she could not stop herself. "You are quite the treasure trove, and I'm sure that there are many women in this town with useful skills who would make an excellent wife for a busy man such as yourself."

"And I am certain there are wealthier men with better prospects who would make an admirable husband for you."

Both of them sat in silence, knowing what they had just said was true. There were dozens of men who would be better suited to keep a wife. There were also dozens of women who were better suited to be a helpmeet who did not wish for so much independence.

Rowena thought of the happiest couple she had ever seen. Her parents.

Would her parents, so suitably matched in happiness, have been happier with one of the more "suitable candidates"? Her father was English and had held a job in London. His family hadn't been pleased when he went to Boston on business, met a beautiful

American, and married her. Granny Nesbitt still had a grudge against the English. She didn't want her daughter marrying anyone but sturdy Massachusetts stock. (Even Connecticut men were deemed unworthy by Granny.) Rowena's hand fell from her lap and landed against Augustus'. Both of them jumped and sprang apart, pressing into the sides of the wicker glider once again.

"Mr. Warwick? You must have little time to read," she ventured, her faint voice almost drowned out by the gentle rustle of the leaves in the night breeze.

"That is true," he admitted, "but I do *like* to read. I just prefer to use my time in making things. Fixing things. Instruments. Bicycles. Sweets." Augustus stopped and twisted his hat in both hands.

Rowena smiled. Mr. Warwick might find it unseemly to speak so freely. Perhaps the strict Colonel Warwick would have told him he was babbling. Whatever it was, she found it charming and not in the least off-putting.

"I wonder if you'd like to accompany Miss Earnshaw, Professor Trilby, and myself to a gathering this Saturday evening? I hear it is to be an evening of poetry, spiritual readings, and musical reflections before Easter?"

"Oh? Me? I-I would be delighted." Augustus stumbled over his acceptance. "Only…Well, are you attending as the guest of Professor Trilby?" He arched one eyebrow. "I would not like to impose."

"No. It is open to all."

Augustus hesitated.

Rowena rose from the glider and leaned against one of the porch's pillars, facing the silent street. "He called Tiger quite a rude name the other day," she told the empty air.

In a moment, Augustus leaned on the opposing pillar, eyes sparkling in the moonlight. "What time shall I meet you?"

****

Rowena's heart floated after Augustus bid her good night. She had met a man in whom she could confide, whom Tiger seemed to like. Carrie Earnshaw seemed to like him. He shared her love of music and her burden of being slightly out of step with the rest of their town.

In the next moment her heart sank. Was she being foolish by getting her hopes up? She and Augustus barely knew one another. So much of her favorable opinion was based on casual observation and a few positive interactions.

But she could certainly observe him for an extended period of time at close range…if she wanted.

****

Augustus opened the store to find a black cat looming on his sidewalk. "It's not that I'm not fond of you, Tiger—" He sighed, welcoming the cat in with a sweep of his arm. "—but I do think your mistress would like you to spend *some* time at home! Besides, haven't you had quite enough of the menfolk of Cedar Point trying to decorate you like a prancing Christmas pony?"

Ignoring his words, the cat boldly prowled into the shop and settled itself in front of the licorice drops.

Augustus frowned. "Yesterday, you didn't like those. Well, I suppose you are entitled to change your mind. Here, try these. They're much softer." He took out several of the licorice jelly beans he had made yesterday. The cat delicately nibbled them from between its front paws, its blue eyes blinking up at him. "Blue eyes?"

Augustus murmured aloud. "Blue eyes? I could have sworn—" He bent closer and found himself facing a black blur.

As suddenly as the cat had arrived, it departed. Augustus heard a scuffle outside on the sidewalk.

"Catch it! Catch it, boys! Five dollars for anyone who can bring me that cat!"

Augustus groaned. He would have recognized Matthew Raine's voice anywhere after hearing far too much of it in the past week.

"I lost that little beggar once, and I'm not going to do it again." Raine laughed raucously.

Hang good service. Hang the unwillingness to offend one of the wealthiest men in town.

Augustus raced out of his shop in time to see Matthew and a few of his employees from the mill flanking him as they chased Tiger down Turnbridge Alley. Quick as a wink, Augustus shot back inside the store, hopped the candy counter, and flew to the back entrance that opened into the tiny, cobbled alley. He whistled and hoped that Tiger was as clever as he thought. In a split second, a black furry blur came shooting down the alley and through his ankles.

"Where is it? Where did it go?" Raine came running along, his silk vest rumpled and his polished patent leather hair escaping its neat part.

"What are you looking for, Matthew? Another valve for your bicycle?" Augustus asked. In the dark of the shop, he saw a flash of brilliant blue before it was swallowed up in shadow. *Clever Tiger.* The cat was blending in with the darkness of his workshop.

"That horrible cat of Rowena Mumford's," Matthew hissed, his handsome features turning brick red. A scowl twisted his face until it was quite grotesque, like some evil satyr's. "I've got a plan for it this time." Matthew pulled a tiny vial out of his waistcoat pocket. "Two of my mother's sleeping tablets. Crushed up and mixed with a little milk. I'll put that on the creature's tongue. I figure it'll just be waking up by the time I present it to Miss Mumford, complete with a shiny new bell."

"That's cheating." Augustus smiled grimly.

"I don't think so," Matthew said, popping the vial back in his pocket with a shrug. "I never heard anyone say we couldn't drug the little beast. I only heard them say we had to have a bell around its neck. Rowena Mumford wants to play this damn silly game, let her! I'll play it, and I'll win it."

Augustus tried to hold his tongue. Memories of last night's companionable silence, followed by easy conversation, made such a feat impossible. "Matthew, why in God's name do you want a wife you have to trick? You are a wealthy man, and half the women in Cedar Point would be delighted to marry you. What do you even fancy about Rowena Mumford?"

Matthew Raine stopped skulking around, taken aback. "Auggie," he exclaimed softly, "I've never heard you say that many words in my life. Well, it's a question worth asking. You always were the curious sort. Frankly, it's none of your concern, but I don't mind telling you. Mumford is a beautiful woman with no family of her own. My family is large, and my mother's been wanting grandchildren. Think of all the things that I could give her. A home, stability, *respectability*…Those tiresome rumors about witchcraft would stop for a start."

"True," Augustus admitted, half to himself.

Matthew continued. "Since she's alone, her family

money could go into the Raine family coffers, and all of her beauty can go into my sons and daughters. Don't look so shocked, old man, she'll get just as good as she gives. She'll have a future in this town, wealth, privilege, and success for her children and mine. Her cat can have its own little island if that will make her happy. Any wife and children of mine will live in luxury."

Augustus swallowed. He could never promise the same thing, and it was none of his concern. Nonetheless, he asked, "What if she can't have children?"

Matthew gasped, looking horrified. "Bite your tongue. That's a question for medical men, Augustus, not for the tinkers and piano tuners of the world."

"I only ask because it seems like you want her for the things she can *give* you, not for the woman herself."

Matthew hesitated. He was clearly unused to being questioned, and he didn't think much of it. "I have a number of reasons why the woman would be enough exactly as she is, but they're all private and none of your concern." Raine gave Augustus an unmistakable leer. "As any man ought to know."

"Thinking of the unexpected things in life doesn't make you less of a man."

"Says a man who spends his time among pianos and toffees," scoffed Raine.

"What you're looking for isn't here, so happy hunting," Augustus said abruptly. He consoled himself that he wasn't really telling a lie. Rowena wasn't here, just her cat, and it sounded like Matthew wanted no part of it.

"Right, I'll try around the lake. The confounded beast is always chasing the ducks. Oh, Augustus, you won't tell anyone about my little plan, will you?" Raine patted his pocket.

Augustus stared him down without speaking. With a cough, Matthew left, rallying his workers with a loud cry.

"All right, Tiger," Augustus whispered once he had shut and bolted the back door, casting the workshop into an even deeper darkness. "If I were you, I'd stay here for the day where someone can look after you. Matthew Raine is out there with his money, paying people to do his dirty work. To him, there's nothing unfair about how he catches you. The only thing that matters is that he does. Here." Augustus found the cat rubbing along his shins, and he bent to stroke its silky ears. "You take a nap on my tool bag. You seemed to like that the other day. If you're going to leave, come out through the front of the store, and run straight home." He put his hands on his hips and spoke to the cat as if it were a naughty child. "Oh, heavens. I'm glad no one else heard that. As if a cat can understand all of that!"

Still…Augustus could have sworn it winked at him as he headed back to his kitchen.

****

Rowena always kept a spare set of clothing in the little potting shed in her garden. That afternoon, she streaked into it with only a few moments to spare before her first piano lesson of the day.

Breath spasmed from her body as she transformed, not from the exertion of shifting forms or from the fact that she'd run a good two miles without stopping. She was seething with indignation. Matthew Raine was trying to drug her. Other men were laying snares for her! Well, for Tiger, but regardless, she felt it was dangerous and cruel. If she weren't actually a human in disguise, she wondered what would have become of her. She knew Tiger was a very clever cat, but would he have heard and understood phrases such as "That big brute can't resist a nice chunk of salted cod. Mr. Raine poured sleeping powder over it?"

After Rowena's jaunt in disguise, she learned that most men in town were no longer pursuing her for their own desires but were acting on behalf of Matthew Raine. He had promised them money for catching the cat and money on top of their wages for putting in hours outside the mill. Unfortunately, this meant that the questionable and cruel methods she'd observed could all be attributed to Matthew Raine's obsession with making her his bride.

She would have to call off this farce.

Unless there was another option…

Shivering into her dress despite the warmth of April in the cozy darkened shed, Rowena remembered the way Augustus stroked her spine and fondled her ears. It was not to be taken as anything more than a simple gesture of kindness to an animal, of course, but the fact that she was the one disguised as the animal meant she'd experienced the tenderness of his touch and appreciated it. She also endured the crippling grasp and the clutching fingers of Matthew Raine and his mill workers. They thought it was a lark to try to catch the cat in any way they could, and if it hurt the animal, so be it.

She'd started this foolishness. She had to finish it before someone got hurt.

Matrimony might be the only way to solve the problem.

"Smartest woman in town? Ha." With a groan, she stalked into the house, vowing that she and Tiger would stay inside as much as possible.

Chapter Eleven

"Son? Augustus? Well, I hope you're in. You shouldn't go leaving your business unattended like that."

Augustus finished knotting his tie and using the stiffest horsehair bristle brush he could find to force his brazen curls into order. "Yes, I'm home, Father. Also, the store isn't unattended, the sign on the shop said 'Closed.' "

The sound of creaking joints and clacking walking stick accompanied a huffy groan. "Then your door ought to be locked."

"It can't be locked if I intend to go through it." August trotted down the stairs from his flat and through the workshop, careful not to smudge his good fawn-colored suit on any of his half-finished projects.

Colonel Warwick stared, open-mouthed. "Augustus! Augustus, my lad. You look…what's happened? Who passed away?" The look of surprise rapidly turned to one of worry.

"I'm not attending a funeral service; I'm heading to a literary soiree. A symposium. Simon Trilby will be there."

"You wouldn't dress like that for Simon Trilby." His father shook his head with a chuckle. "Great Scott, your hair. It's flat!"

"Hush, it'll hear you," Augustus grumbled. "Rowena Mumford and Carrie Earnshaw will be accompanying us. I'm dressing for the occasion."

His father, for the first time in his life, appeared at a loss for words. He flopped into a chair and clasped the knob of his walking stick in both hands, pop-eyed and slack-jawed. "Mumford? And little Caroline Earnshaw?"

"She's not little. She's quite tall, actually." Augustus cautiously put on his hat, as if afraid the slightest weight would send his curls into rebellion.

"You? And Caroline?" His father beamed.

"No, Father, me and no one. Not yet. Can't I go out with a pair of ladies as friends?"

"No. It's not done. And you've never done it before."

"Well, there's a first time for everything." Augustus dangled his key in front of his father's face. "Will you be minding the shop, or shall I lock up?"

****

Rowena had invited Carrie to come over early on Saturday evening so they could await the arrival of Mr. Warwick and Professor Trilby together.

"It's the first time I've ever been out for a social event without Mama and Father," the breathless young lady gasped. "Oh, Miss Mumford. I'm nervous. I'm far too nervous. I'm not good at talking to gentlemen. Mother says it's one of my failings. Aside from my face. And my figure." Her voice was heavy with years of being a disappointment.

"It's Rowena, or shall I call you Miss Earnshaw? And none of those things are failings. You simply haven't met the right gentlemen to talk to...or the right dress and hairstyle to complement your natural beauty. You know...I have some dresses that I haven't hemmed yet. They're too long for me, but they'd be just right for you. I have a cream-colored one that would make you look simply radiant."

"Well." Carrie hesitated, then shook her head. "No. Mama has tried so many styles, and I—"

"You are a persistent young woman. Let's try." Rowena gently encouraged, taking her elbow and leading her up the stairs.

In only thirty minutes, a very different Carrie appeared. Her severe bun was undone, replaced with loose ringlets cascading around a simple knot in the back of her hair. The hard lines of her pale features were softened. The cream dress, topped off with a touch of rouge on her cheeks and a pink cameo at her throat, made her glow like some rosy ethereal being.

Of the two of them, Rowena wanted the girl to shine the brightest. She dressed accordingly. She wore a simple black lace dress with a pearl clasp in her hair. If Mr. Warwick admired her for her personality, then her clothing shouldn't matter.

Hopefully.

"That'll be them!" Carrie gasped as someone rapped on the door. "Or at least, that'll be one of them."

Tiger, who'd been lounging in the entryway, sniffed the air and went running pell-mell into the kitchen.

"I think it's the professor." Rowena smirked. She glided, a black swan leading a timid white dove, and threw open the door. "Professor Trilby, how kind of you to collect us. You know Miss Earnshaw, do you not?"

"Of course, I—uh, I...I've met Miss Earnshaw?" The normally articulate man stumbled over his words and trailed off at the sight of the beauty in white. "*Caroline* Earnshaw?"

"My hair is down," Carrie blurted.

Rowena swallowed a sigh. "Shall we wait in the parlor?"

****

Augustus hopped off his bicycle. Trilby had an open carriage, pulled by a rather gaunt-looking brown gelding. It was tied to the hitching post in front of the Mumford house. It stretched its neck, contentedly cropping the young leaves off the maple tree in front of it.

"Good evening, old fellow." Augustus patted the horse's neck as he rested his bicycle on the other side of the hitching post. "I wish I'd known we were traveling in style. I would have brought you a sugar lump or two. It is my stock-in-trade, after all." With another gentle tap on the horse's withers, Augustus walked up the sunset-colored pavement. The stars were beginning to shine on the horizon line.

He was so busy looking at the beauty of the evening (in an effort to calm his nerves) that he didn't see the obstruction in his path until he tripped over it.

"*Rowr!*"

"Tiger! Sorry." Augustus clambered off his knees, praying his suit wasn't torn.

Tiger, merging with the shadows, licked his side, fixing Augustus with fiery green eyes.

"Green. Not blue." Augustus stopped dusting himself down and stood, staring and frozen.

Rowena Mumford was a clever woman. Augustus gave a low, appreciative chuckle in the dark as he scratched Tiger's head, the cat's long plume of a tail caressing his leg. She wasn't a witch, but by jove, she had something devilish about her. Now he knew her secret, and it only made him admire her more.

The woman had two nearly identical black cats! And if one were caught, she could always put forth the other and claim the suitor had nabbed some stray. She would have all the beaus in Cedar Point in a frenzy while she coolly held the reins.

"Mr. Warwick. There you are." A yellow patch of light spilled onto the walkway as the lady of the house opened the door.

"A pleasure to see you, Miss Mumford." Augustus trotted up the steps and squeezed her hand for a moment longer than he needed, unable to keep the smile off his face. "I've just seen Tiger. Or…whatever you call that one." He winked.

She gaped at him. "Wh-what do you mean?"

Augustus, emboldened by admiration and the prospect of earning her trust by keeping her secret, pulled her from the house and gently let the front door fall shut behind her. "I know, Miss Mumford. I know your secret."

She said nothing, her skin losing its creamy tone and fading to sickly gray, the pallor emphasized by her black dress. With a stagger, she clutched the doorframe, bosom heaving.

"Oh! Oh, please, don't worry. I only just figured it out, and I won't tell a soul. I think it's brilliant!" He squeezed her hands, both of them in both of his. A current of electricity ran up his arms and down his spine. His voice came out in a rush, thin and nearly lost in the dark. "You have all the power, the upper hand. Think what you will of me, I can't deny the thought of Matthew Raine being put in his place by you and your feline friends…" Augustus trailed off, his shoulders shaking with suppressed mirth.

Rowena's color slowly returned, and her blue eyes grew brighter than the stars above. Augustus was aware that they were still holding hands. He deftly tried to disengage them, but Rowena dug her hands in. He could feel the warmth of her fingers, skin to skin. It was practically scandalous, as ladies kept their gloves on in mixed company.

"How did you find out?" Rowena's voice shook.

"A difference of eye color. A difference in taste," Augustus mused. Yes, now that he thought of it, one cat was decidedly more mischievous. Tiger seemed to get into things. The other cat seemed a bit more sedate and content to sit still. Augustus wondered if one cat was a female and one was a male. Yes, now that he truly thought back about it, he had stroked both of them, and there was a difference in the texture of their fur. The blue-eyed cat had smoother fur. It almost felt like human hair, but shorter and thicker.

"Mr. Warwick?"

Augustus patted her hand as he freed his arm from her desperate grasp. "It's only the smallest details. The fur, the eyes, even the size and shape." He shook his head, impressed with her cleverness. "Anyone who *really* paid attention could tell that they're two different cats."

Miss Mumford's eyes had been downcast while he spoke, but now they climbed to meet his face. "You figured out my secret just from observing the two…cats?"

Augustus nodded. "I am an observant man, and I must confess that lately I've been keen to observe everything I can about you."

After a second of hesitation, Rowena rose on the

balls of her feet and dashed a kiss against his cheek. "Why didn't you tell me before?" she whispered.

"That I figured out your secret?" He blinked. "Well, I've only just—"

She cut him off, fingers pressing into his arm. "No, you dear man. That you were keen to—" Rowena stopped, her normally serene, self-assured face as confused as his own. "I find myself at a loss for words."

Augustus pressed a hand to his cheek, bewildered but in a very pleasant way. "Don't fret, Miss Mumford. I don't often speak much myself." Augustus laughed. He swallowed, unable to tune out his father's voice, and for once very glad about it.

You don't need to be a man of words, son. Be a man of action.

His father had wanted him to go bravely into battle.

But this might be more terrifying.

Bending low, Augustus pressed a kiss to Rowena's startled lips, his impertinent hair mingling with her exquisitely arranged coiffure.

Women don't let men kiss them unless they're engaged or nearly so.

What in Heaven's name am I doing?

And why is she kissing me back?

****

Crashing chords. Glittering glissandos. Surging music filled Rowena's ears, but the street was silent, except for the usual early evening noises.

Augustus Warwick knew her secret.

He knew her work habits and her passions.

He knew her favorite candy and how to coax her thoroughly devilish cat into a basket.

Mr. Warwick was the sort of gentleman whose suit

111

she would gladly hear.

When he stopped kissing her, her body prickled as though she were about to go through a transformation, but she didn't.

Magic. Heat. Excitement.

Be careful, Rowena, she urged herself.

"I'm terribly sorry. That was too forward. We're not even courting." Augustus pulled away, flushed and breathing hard.

"I think we are now." She laughed, brazen but uncaring.

"Oh, yes, I—"

"Hasn't Warwick turned up yet?" Simon Trilby poked his head through the door and bumped right into her back. "I beg pardon. *Ohhh.* I…Ah. Miss Earnshaw, shall we go back to discussing my latest article for the *Boston Seminarian*?"

Rowena smoothed her hair with a self-conscious laugh. "No, Professor, no. We must get on. Mr. Warwick has arrived."

I never knew the man I was waiting for lived right here in town…

****

Rowena enjoyed the carriage ride, although she didn't say much. She was watching Carrie and Trilby. The two were talking animatedly, Carrie hanging on every pompous, learned word, while he encouraged her on every reply, laughing and praising her for her astuteness.

She and Augustus exchanged smiles from their places in back, she sitting next to Carrie, and he occupying the other seat alone while the professor held the reins.

"I'll drive us home, Trilby," Augustus offered when the professor stopped talking to catch his breath.

"Yes, and I'll sit with you, Mr. Warwick. I would like to learn how to drive a carriage. I know you've a way with animals," Rowena suggested, her hand briefly resting on his elbow.

"And he has a way with music," Carrie piped up, looking more relaxed and happy than Rowena could ever recall seeing her. "He's a very skillful pianist."

"I would not go that far."

"In my estimation, anyone who can play 'The Maple Leaf Rag' is very talented," Carrie said staunchly.

Rowena turned her head to him so fast that her hair whipped Carrie across the nose. "You like Joplin?"

"Greatly. I have an old upright in the repair shop. 'The Maple Leaf Rag' is my favorite piece to play."

"That ragtime music has a corrupting influence on young people," Trilby called back.

"So does betting," Augustus replied, leaning back in his seat, eyes fixed on the professor's back.

Rowena quite liked the easy confidence he had when he spoke, when he allowed himself to sprawl a bit, clearly willing to challenge the other man's views. But for whatever reason, Trilby said no more on the subject.

Carrie filled the awkward silence. "Oh, I wish you could play for them tonight, Miss Mumford! Reading and music would be such a pleasant way to pass the evening."

"Well, it's in the church hall. There's a piano." Rowena fussed with the shining ebony folds of her skirt. "But I don't like to…I shouldn't like to draw attention to myself."

"Perhaps you ladies would give us a duet? What's

that French piece by Delibes that everyone is going mad for?" Trilby suggested.

" 'The Flower Duet.' " Rowena smiled. She'd performed it in Paris, both as the soprano and as the accompanying pianist. "It is very popular, and for good reason. It's very appropriate for spring and Easter, although the story follows the tale of a Hindu priest's daughter."

"Ah. I was unaware of that. Perhaps it's unsuitable for this evening." A faint note of disapproval could be heard in the professor's single syllable.

"I have the greatest respect for the people of India and their culture. I disapprove of the way in which the people of Great Britain have tried to impose their will on the Indian people instead of trying to form an equitable trading treaty. My parents had dear friends in Pondicherry and among all the different castes." Rowena's voice hardened, losing its usual soft demure tones, most unbecoming to a woman. Carrie looked torn between admiration and shock.

Mr. Warwick simply looked amused.

Before Professor Trilby could remark further, Rowena concluded, speaking much more softly, "Not only that, but Miss Earnshaw and I often concluded our French lessons by singing. That was one of our favorites, wasn't it, Carrie?"

"But we never sang in front of anyone," Carrie croaked. "Besides, you played the piano, Miss Mumford. We haven't an accompanist, and it would look like a music hall show for a woman to sit and sing while playing." The younger woman's face was whiter than her gown, eyes darting toward the disapproving back of Professor Trilby.

"I'll play for you," Mr. Warwick said suddenly.

"What?" Rowena turned surprised eyes from her companion to the man she'd kissed.

"I'll play for you and Miss Earnshaw. I'm a dab hand at the piano...but I'm hopeless at French. You sing. I'll play." He smiled reassuringly, nodding several times.

"But—we don't have the music. Carrie and I've never practiced with an accompanist other than myself."

"Trust me."

Rowena's throat moved, but no sound came out. If she could trust Augustus with her most terrible secret, surely she could trust him at the piano?

****

Rowena was surprised at how full the church hall was. Perhaps she should not have been, as the Cedar Point Episcopal Church had been the heart and soul of the community since the town was founded. Even those who were not ardently faithful would attend social functions either out of a desire to appear well-heeled and respectable or from sheer boredom in a town that did not boast a library, a theater, or a music hall. She was not surprised to see that it was mainly full of young people. There were those who were newly married or without children, and the courting couples who sat a respectable foot apart in the pews. Filling the front pews in a chattering throng were the "educated men" and the young seminarians who always sat in the back of Wilder's Bookshop and debated worldly affairs while their pipes turned the air a sweet smoky gray.

Rowena felt all eyes upon her and Augustus. In the past, she would have said it was her and her alone that they were gawking at, but walking in the company of Carrie and Mr. Warwick changed that. Perhaps they were staring at plain, quiet Carrie Earnshaw who entered their midst like a cherub minus wings. Or perhaps it was the sight of Mr. Warwick laughing and chatting gaily, another man who kept himself to himself. The three of them sat in a pew towards the back of the room. Simon, however, headed to the front of the sanctuary, head held high and clearly holding court among his peers, colleagues, and even a few of his pupils.

In moments, the gathering switched from a casual conversation to a structured program, led off by Trilby himself. Rowena sank back against the hard wood of the long, polished pew. Beside her, Carrie leaned forward, eyes wide as Trilby orated, strutting around the pulpit, impassioned words pouring from his mouth.

"He's wonderful," Carrie whispered breathlessly.

"I think he's pleased to have such an attentive audience." Augustus leaned across Rowena to smile at the woman in white.

While Carrie leaned forward, more and more enamored with every passing second, Rowena sank into a stupor, words washing over her. Eventually, she was aware that the speaker changed and kept changing, a smattering of women in an ocean of men.

At last, as the church bell was tolling nine, Professor Trilby made his way to the front of the church. "We have with us tonight Cedar Point's most prominent piano teacher and piano repairman, as well as the very talented recent applicant to Radcliffe, Carrie Earnshaw."

Rowena and Augustus exchange a sly smile. Trilby had clearly decided he favored Carrie, and the admiration was mutual.

During the polite applause, Rowena rose, flanked by a trembling Carrie. She had no doubt that she and Carrie could sing beautifully together as this was one of their favorite pieces, a French duet for two female voices. Could Augustus keep up? Was he indeed the trustworthy person he claimed to be?

"Miss Mumford, you are as white as a ghost." Carrie was equally pale as she clasped her teacher's elbow.

"It is the lighting of this hall." Rowena stumbled as all the eyes in the room turned toward her.

"May I?" Augustus offered her his elbow. She took it, her smooth fingers taking comfort in someone else's touch, comfort in his unshakable solid warmth.

A titter of shocked commentary ran around the pews. Rowena realized that tongues would wag as she let herself lean on him, the picture of a courting couple. A handsome couple. She knew others thought her beautiful, and Augustus…How were the girls of Cedar Point restraining themselves? Perhaps they'd never realized how dashing he was, hidden behind his pots and pans, his axles and tires. Mentally, she changed his heather tweeds and her black dress to bridal white and morning suit.

Not to be outdone, Trilby rushed to take Miss Earnshaw's elbow and escort her to a place beside the spinet.

Rowena held her breath as Augustus sat down at the piano. She had never heard him play more than a few chords at a time, testing the sound of his tuning. She tried to smile as she faced the audience, but instead her mouth dropped open in a very unladylike fashion. Augustus' fingers nimbly danced across the keys in a perfect rendition of "The Flower Duet's" opening measures. She cast a sideways glance at Carrie to see if the girl looked shocked or nervous, but instead the young woman looked quite smug. On her, it turned out to be a very fetching look, giving her an air of womanly confidence. Trilby thought so too, if his riveted expression was any clue.

Carrie nudged her discreetly, white elbow digging into black ribs. As if this had all been rehearsed a thousand times, Rowena started to sing. Her higher soprano merged beautifully with Carrie's rich mezzo soprano tones. She dared not look back at Augustus for long, but when she did, the look he was giving her made everything in her body simmer. Notes came out more passionately, spurred on by the heat in his gaze. She barely remembered herself singing, more enchanted with the fact that Augustus Warwick never even looked at his hands. He was playing the entire complicated accompaniment by ear, with eyes only for her.

A partner, she thought, *in more ways than one.*

****

"Ah, Warwick!" Trilby flung his arm out as he leaned back against the carriage seats. "Are we not the two luckiest men in the city? Or perhaps the entire state?"

"If you refer to the quality of our company, Trilby, then I say we are the two luckiest men in the nation, if not the world. Where else could a man find such exquisite companionship?"

"Beautiful of face as well as voice," Trilby praised, scooting nearer than was strictly gentlemanly. Carrie giggled.

Rowena was likewise squeezed close to Augustus' side as they shared the driver's seat.

When she'd attended school in Paris, she'd seen women who were far more brazen. Sweethearts kissed in the parks and on the bridges while she was supposed to be sketching and mastering watercolors. It was shocking to her, a girl who had spent most of her life in reserved Cedar Point where affection was kept behind closed doors.

Hadn't she been just as bold as those passionate Parisiennes? Would her parents be ashamed of her for kissing Augustus so impulsively? Or would they be grateful that she'd finally found someone after years alone?

From the back of the coach, Rowena heard the professor's voice drop an octave, now low and rustling. With her unusually fine hearing, she could still catch the conversation.

"May I call upon you sometime, Miss Earnshaw?"

"Professor, I am intending to spend the fall at Radcliffe, should I be accepted."

"While I intend to spend the summer in Cape Cod. But we have the spring, do we not? One may hope to correspond."

"Indeed, we could. One learns so much about the other person that way. Why, epistles are even in the Bible."

"If it is good enough for our Lord and Savior and His apostles, then surely it should be good enough for the two of us," Trilby concluded with a laugh.

"How are things progressing with your jellied sweets, Mr. Warwick?" Rowena's voice was too loud in her own ears, ruining the lover-like whispers she'd overheard.

"I've perfected their construction, but I now have to produce them in quantity. I should be busy right up until Easter. Although my Sunday afternoons are always free."

Rowena swallowed, searching for a reply that would balance the rebellious heat in her middle with the notions of proprietary in her head. "If your shop would welcome the occasional patron before your normal opening hours, I could use a quiet place to do some of my writing. It is very convenient to the post office."

Had he been proposing Sunday afternoon outings?

Had she been too forward in suggesting they meet more often?

"It's noisy in the shop."

"Even with no one else there?" Oh, dear. That sounded *much* too bold.

His voice was a deep, licorice-black timbre that made her pulse pound, that called out to something in her, that little slip of animal hiding under a pretty face. "Well, if you proposed visiting the shop before ten, Miss Mumford, you'll find me frantically banging about making all the sweets, roasting the nuts, and what have you."

"Ah."

"But you'd be very welcome. After all, your *cat* is there more often than not these days."

"Tiger is very fond of you." She leaned her head close to his shoulder, able to inhale the scent of him...chocolate and salt, fruit and mint. Her mouth watered, her appetite, merely functional for the past six years, returned with a sudden vengeance. "And so is the *other one*."

"Have a care, Warwick, you nearly drove us off the street!"

"I was distracted," Augustus replied, clucking his tongue at the horse. "Sorry, old fellow."

"Blame me." Rowena laughed.

"I credit you, Miss Mumford. For ever so many things," Carrie sighed in a dreamy voice. "What a splendid night."

In the darkness, all four members of the party beamed in agreement.

Chapter Twelve

The next week was idyllic. Each morning, Rowena, often followed by Tiger, sat alone at the table closest to the sweet shop counter. Tiger rested in a patch of sun in the middle of the floor. Rowena wrote and sometimes embroidered (which gave her an excuse to watch Augustus in his kitchen).

Augustus' father, Colonel Warwick, began coming to the shop to sit at a table on the opposite side of the shop, clearing his throat and nodding gruffly, saying little after his initial greeting. Augustus whistled and clanked as he banged his way through the morning's preparations. Her mouth watered both from the way he simply accepted her in companionable silence as well as from the heavenly aromas he produced.

Every day she left as the crowds of Main Street clerks swarmed out at noon. She had afternoon lessons to give and papers to post. Tiger usually sauntered home after her, causing some of the older women of the town to cluck their tongues and whisper behind their hands about Rowena being one of the devil's own.

She didn't care. Not in six years had she been so blissfully content.

Was this love?

Possibly.

Happiness?

Most definitely.

****

"I heard you caused quite a stir with her the other night." Colonel Warwick waited until the noon rush subsided and took a place at the counter, surprising Augustus. "Salted nuts, please. An assortment."

"If we caused a stir, it was merely musical, Father." Augustus filled up a paper sack and considered putting a price to his offering. At the last moment, kindness won out over years of badgering, and he slipped his father an extra scoop.

"You'll never make a profit that way, boy," the colonel exclaimed. "Tell me what I owe you."

Augustus sighed. "Twenty cents, and if you want to take Mother home something, it'll be another twenty. Don't fret, I'll pick it out with my profit margins in mind."

"Good lad. Smart thinking. That Mumford woman…" He twirled the brassy knob of his walking stick against his palm, thoughtfully sucking his teeth. "She's quite the thoughtful sort. And must have a good head for figures. Doesn't run to extravagance, not that I can see. Keeps her family home going. Unusually gifted."

Augustus smiled. "Yes." *Unusual* was the perfect word for Rowena. Unusually gifted, beautiful, and sweet. Unusually happy to be by his side, not making demands. Happiness and contentment washed over him, seeping in bone-deep. He doubted whether even his father could shatter this moment.

"You fancy her, Augustus?" The colonel's voice was softer than Augustus could ever recall hearing it.

"Ah. Yes." Augustus sighed a lover's sigh that would have done any Romeo proud. "Indeed, I do."

"Word has gotten round town that there are matches in the offing. Trilby's calling at the Earnshaw house each night. Wolfgang Ruger hired a seamstress and has started seeing her home each night. He's even asked her round for Easter luncheon." Colonel Warwick's mustache danced.

"Father, you are becoming as gossipy as any old fishwife. In fact, the fishmonger's wife is remarkably silent on the subject."

"She doesn't know you like I do." The old soldier limped stiffly to his feet, his spine straightening as he assumed command position. "It seems that you and the Mumford girl are strangely suited. But don't make a hash of it the way you usually do. Tinkering about. Pottering. You'll think everything is wrapped up in a pretty bow, the ink is dry, the t's are crossed…And by jove, she'll be marrying that rich boy, Matthew Raine, before you blink. You'll have assumed things were all sorted, and the job would be half finished." The colonel paced, raking one hand through his normally tidy gray hair. "You do this, Augustus. You start one job and leave it to tinker on another. When inspiration strikes you, you move toward it. That's why you don't have one successful business, you have three."

Augustus frowned. "Surely that's a good thing? I have three successful businesses, any one of them could earn a living." His father gave him a long-suffering glare. Augustus flushed. "Sort of." Only the sweet shop earned enough to be considered a proper profession. The other two made a nice bit of income, but it was not steady. "It's better to have my finger in several pies than none."

"Rowena Mumford won't think so. She'll want a man who's not too busy to court her! You haven't asked her to go on an outing with you."

Augustus winced. Even though it was true, he didn't like how his father had stated it as a fact.

"It is not proper that a woman should have to do all the pursuing, son."

Augustus let out a startled bleat as he realized that his fresh batch of strawberry syrup was about to boil over. His father gave him a knowing glance.

"You see? Distracted."

"Yes, at the moment I'm distracted by you," Augustus hissed, burning his fingers as he vigorously whisked the sticky concoction down.

"All I want to do is make sure you don't let this opportunity pass you by. Like West Point."

He bit down a groan. "I will call her on Sunday afternoon. It's all arranged." Augustus crossed his fingers behind the counter where his father couldn't see him. The part about Sunday afternoon was true enough, but he had no idea what they would do together.

"About time. Now, pay attention to her, Augustus, and only her. I don't want to hear that you took her for a jaunt in that benighted bicycle-wagon of yours and then abandoned her when you remembered that you left the stove on."

"The jelly beans! I meant to start the next batch of lemon." Augustus fled to the back of the shop.

Behind him, he heard his father grumbling a prayer. "Dear Lord…could You at least let the boy remember to bring her flowers or sweets? He does have a fair supply."

"Amen," Augustus muttered.

****

"Wh-what would you like to do this afternoon, Miss Mumford?"

Rowena stepped back into her house, beckoning her suitor in. *My suitor. I have a suitor.*

He shouldn't be alone in the house with me.

But he already has been, time and again, every year since I've lived alone.

Augustus hesitated in the doorway, then followed her in. "It's a gorgeous day. We could go to the pond. The park?"

She wanted to stay inside, alone, and talk. To ask him questions about himself. Questions like, "Why doesn't my ability to turn into a feline spook you?"

Instead, she blundered into the coat closet, banging her hip on the door handle. "Ah—we could play croquet?"

"Croquet?" Augustus repeated.

"I have the hoops and mallets. The lawn isn't prepared but..." Rowena trailed off with a shrug. "We could play a few rounds before tea. W-would you like to stay for tea?"

"Splendid." Augustus strode forward, then stopped. "Forgive me, but I assumed you would want to go out someplace."

She was too old and too used to loneliness to mince words. "I'm in no need of a chaperone, Mr. Warwick. If I didn't think you could be trusted with my 'virtue,' you wouldn't come in to tune my piano. As for what the wagging tongues will say..." Her eyes drifted over Augustus' face. "The rumors aren't exactly true, but they're true enough, aren't they?"

"Your dear little 'witch's familiar'? Hello, Tiger." He stooped to stroke the cat.

Rowena shook her head, eyes suddenly glistening. "You may joke, but—"

"Rowena, you know what they say about me." Augustus gripped her elbow, pulling her back as she stepped away. "Crackpot. Fool. Dreamer. Worse. In this town, calling a man an idle failure and a disappointment is every bit as bad as calling a woman a witch."

"Outcast. They have a word for it in India." Her throat slid shut, letting out a tiny whisper as she realized her chest had somehow pressed to his. " 'Untouchable.' "

His hand flexed on her arm, twitching as he licked his lips. "We seem to…we seem to be able to touch."

"Augustus…" Why was the room darkening, turning into nothingness, her eyes only able to see him?

"These last weeks have been a dream, and this last week the sweetest dream of all. I don't feel out of place around you," he confessed, head dipping.

She rose on her tiptoes, chin tilted up to his. "We seem to fit together."

And then they did, lips perfectly matched.

So perfectly matched…

Chapter Thirteen

"Most lovers court in the dark of night, but I woo my love before noon. I'll woo her in the morning light, not by the light of the moon. One day I'll ask her to be my wife…Wait." Augustus stopped singing in his empty shop, searching for a rhyme. "One day I'll ask her to be my wife, and that day is coming soon? One day I'll ask her to be my wife, and we'll wed in June? Soon, June, loon…Just as well that Rowena isn't here for this performance."

Humming his little ditty, Augustus polished "Rowena's table." Every morning around nine, she tapped at the door, Tiger at her heels or popping his head out of the basket over her arm. He welcomed her in with a bow before escorting her to the corner of the shop behind her preferred seat.

"Good morning, Miss Mumford."

"It's Rowena," she would return, before slipping her arms around his waist.

"Good morning, Rowena." He would kiss her.

And that was courting. An everyday greeting before they began their daily tasks, working at parallel lives, side by side. The conversation flowed until the shop was busy—and the shop was at its peak! News of "Easter baskets" had spread, little ones adored the samples of jelly beans he was giving out, and half of Cedar Point came into gawk at the candymaker and the writing woman. Half of the time, his father joined the throng at the shop. Augustus was pleased to see that the colonel silently gave off a disapproving air if anyone stared for too long as Rowena's pen danced across the paper. Should any of the men in town start snickering and muttering about the folly of a woman writing anything beyond a grocer's list, Warwick Sr. would be on his feet, eyes like flint and his walking stick thumping a warning.

But Sunday was the best. Sunday was croquet in the back garden, kissing far too many times, then a stroll some place, and then dinner.

Simple.

Simply heaven.

"Augustus?" Rowena rapped at the door, startling him out of his happy reverie.

"Miss Mumford." Augustus rushed to greet her, a smile filling his face and his heart. He all but pulled her in and didn't even wait until they were in the corner (which was out of view of the wide display window) to kiss her beautiful, beaming lips.

"Mr. Warwick," she gasped.

Augustus turned his eyes to the street, and sure enough, a handful of people were passing by. "Oh, dear. I suppose they saw."

"I suppose they did." Rowena gave a despairing sigh. "I shall need a scarlet letter for my handbag."

"No, you shall not! Courting couples…well, engaged couples…hr-hrm." Augustus coughed. For all his singing about wooing and weddings, he hadn't said anything formal to Rowena. He supposed he should wait. After all, one didn't rush a woman to the altar.

"Engaged?" Rowena looked at him, blue eyes wide and hypnotic.

"Would you have Easter supper with my parents? I'll be there, too. Of course." He winced.

"I would love to. But I was going to ask if you'd like to have Easter luncheon with my family. My cousin Isabelle and my grandmother."

"I would be delighted. Couldn't we do both? Your cousin is Isabelle Browne, and you're Mildred Nesbitt's granddaughter. Both homes are only a mile or two from my parents'."

"It's at Isabelle's house."

Silence.

Nodding.

"I've never been very good at working on a conventional timeline." Augustus pulled out her chair and sat across from her.

"No?"

As soon as his backside touched the chair, he sprang out of it, nervous energy buzzing through his legs as he paced. He was happy Tiger had stayed home, or he was sure the cat would have tripped him as it wound through his ankles. "This Saturday would make three weeks of official courtship. If you consider our first outing the night at the church hall—"

"I would. But we've been associates for quite a lot longer. We were schoolchildren together, though a few years apart."

"That's another thing. Aren't I considered a tradesman? I come to tune your piano."

"Aren't I rather a bad catch?" she countered, blue eyes flashing up at him with a mixture of amusement and annoyance. "I'm an old maid."

"Nonsense."

"I think a lot of customs around marriage are

nonsense. So much has to do with the suitability of circumstances and less about the suitability of souls. Earthly riches fade and beauty withers. I'd rather have a man who is dear to me, whatever his age or class." Rowena paused, biting her lower lip. "Although you are not a tradesman, Augustus. You are an entrepreneur, an inventor, a musician...and most of all, a friend."

"I'd rather hoped that Miss Earnshaw was your friend and I was a bit more." He sank back into the seat and took her hands, her periwinkle-blue-gloved fingers slipping easily between his. "Rowena, I..." Augustus' tongue froze in mid speech. Who would he ask for permission to wed her? She had no father and no grandfather. Perhaps some patriarchal relative remained in England?

"What is it?"

"If, in time, I were to inquire about..." He was captured by her blue eyes again. Something wriggled in the back of his memory, and he blurted, "Why doesn't the other cat show up in my store?"

"Oh. The *other* cat. She...prefers only to be seen at home. I suppose...I suppose that is something that you really need to know about before you consider or inquire about anything like matrimony." Rowena nodded, her chin set. She pulled her hands from his and rose.

Augustus stood, startled. Well, he supposed he should get to be friends with the more elusive, less mischievous black cat, but it was hardly grounds for ending a courtship or planning a wedding. "Did I say something wrong? Please tell me honestly, it wouldn't be surprising. My father would insist it is my normal state, to say the wrong thing at the wrong time."

"No! No, it's perfectly normal you should wonder.

I'll show you tonight. Will you come over once the shop is closed? I know it'll be late, but—"

"I would come over at midnight, should you ask me. I would do anything for you. Rowena, I...I know it's too soon to say this, but as I just said, I'm no good at timing, unless we're speaking of confections or music." He ran his hands past hers, up her arms, sliding her deeper into his embrace.

"Your timing is wonderful. Just tell me."

"I l—"

"So! It's true."

Augustus turned from Rowena as if his shirttail were on fire.

"Mr. Raine." Rowena nodded to the handsome man standing in the shop doorway.

A sneer twisted his features as he strode in. "Miss Mumford, I'd heard that you were seen in an indelicate position, in broad daylight, no less."

"Indelicate? Why, surely you are not so old-fashioned as to think a woman may not embrace her sweetheart?" Rowena smiled and slipped her arm possessively through Augustus' elbow.

"Sweetheart?"

Augustus snorted a laugh that he turned into a cough. Matthew Raine resembled a handsome halibut more than a man at the moment, with pop eyes, glistening, graying skin, and a gaping mouth. "You're here early, Raine. Can I get you something? Chocolates? Bicycle parts?"

"The cat. Where's the cat?"

"At home, sleeping," Rowena replied.

"But the bell..." Matthew spluttered.

"Mr. Warwick has already mastered that part of the

courtship. He could dress Tiger up in booties and a baby bonnet if he had a mind to." Rowena grinned up at her swain, patting his elbow with pride. "He'd never try to drug an innocent animal nor set teams of men to chase a poor creature throughout town."

Matthew's eyes narrowed to menacing slits. "You told her, Warwick. You told her about the sleeping tablets."

"I did no such thing. I've never breathed a word about your foul plots and underhanded methods." Augustus pushed himself away from Rowena and marched up to Raine. "Perhaps if you hadn't set half the men at the mill to cat-hunting, word wouldn't have gotten around."

"Augustus didn't need to disparage you in order to win my heart," Rowena chimed in, a pitying smile on her features as she looked at Matthew. He was now the image of an overgrown toddler, puffing and red-faced, eyes scrunched up in anger. "I prefer his company to yours, Mr. Raine. I'm sure there are many women who would find your company preferable to Mr. Warwick's."

Augustus was sure Rowena's words were true, but he couldn't deny feeling a bit slighted. Until she came to stand beside him again, looking up at him adoringly.

"That's fine by me," she murmured, "for I want him all to myself."

"I love you, Rowena." Augustus didn't know the words would slip out, or that she'd say them back. Everything was a haze of sweet scents and her slipping back into his arms. He was dimly aware of Matthew Raine storming out of the shop, banging the door behind him.

****

"I told him I loved him. I kissed him. In front of Matthew Raine, that odious man." Rowena sat at the piano. Tiger perched on top of it, nibbling the edge of her sheet music. "I think he wants to marry me, Tiger. I want to marry him. I know it's too quick, too soon, but...well, in the Bible, Isaac knew he wanted Rebekah from the moment she watered his camels. Do you think it would be too much for the Lord to let me know I wanted to marry Mr. Warwick from the moment he brought my cat home in a picnic hamper?"

"Mrrrrp," Tiger answered while jumping lightly to the floor.

"But he needs to know how my 'affliction' works. I suppose it's only fair. He asked why he never sees the other cat, and so... and so I told him I'd show him." Rowena's hands fell to the keys with a jangle of notes. Her head rested on the wooden music stand above, her eyes closed. "What if I lose him when he sees it's true? He says he knows my secret, he must've..." Rowena wondered again when he might have seen her transform.

A hot flush of embarrassment slid up her body. He couldn't have seen her transform from human to cat, for that she always did in the house or in the potting shed. It wouldn't have been such a mortifying occurrence either, to see a dress slowly emptying until it was a puddle of fabric, a cat slipping out of its folds. But if he caught the other end of the transformation? Watching a cat turn into a woman who needed to hurry into her dress?

Rowena groaned. The thought of intimacy was exciting, but she'd prefer it to be mutual.

"Enough of that. I've at least soured Mr. Raine on the idea of catching you or me. You should have seen his face. If looks could kill, you'd be on your way to Granny

Nesbitt's. Ahh, and if you could have seen Augustus' face when I said I didn't want to share him. Oh, Tiger. I don't care if it's too soon." Rowena rose abruptly and scooped up the cat, whirling it with her as she waltzed happily in her parlor. "I make him happy. He makes me happy. We're not alone anymore. And he likes animals. Perhaps you'll finally get a real kitten to keep you company."

****

"Flowers. Chocolates. Courage. String." Augustus parked his bicycle (the one without a wagon behind it) against the porch steps.

"Good evening, Mr. Warwick." Rowena opened the door before he reached it. "What pretty lilies."

"For you. And chocolates. I'm trying to court you properly." Augustus knew he shouldn't tell the woman he was wooing his plans, but yet, Rowena was also his friend. He laughed, suddenly at ease simply because she was near him. "I even brought some string for the cats. What do you call the other one?"

Rowena ushered him inside and took his coat and hat. "Tiger, if I have to explain."

"Ah. Smart! So no one else knows. Tiger and Tigress at home?" He smiled and she blushed.

"I suppose Tigress might be appropriate at home," she conceded. "My parents saw tigers in India. They're fierce. They swim, you know. They're unique, not like other cats. The people of India believe the goddess Durga rides upon a tiger. She's the mother goddess, you might say. She and the tiger represent the sacred power of women. They believe Durga and the tiger are fearless and fight evil."

Augustus nodded, bespelled. When Rowena spoke,

it was like listening to music. He found himself lost in the rhythm of her words, desperate to hear more. "What else do they believe about tigers?"

"Well, some tribes in the north country believe man and tiger are brothers. They would never kill a tiger, and the tigers guard the villages from the other beasts in the jungle. So…the idea of man and tiger, or human and cat being related, it's nothing out of the ordinary there. Hm. Once, my mother saved the life of a cat. And it in turn saved her. That's what started this…situation."

"Hm? What situation? The situation with Tiger and Tigress?" Augustus blinked himself out of his stupor, watching as Rowena moved through the parlor, glowing in the lamplight.

"Yes. She had the affliction, too. The ability, I suppose. Some would say it's evil, but I only use it for good."

"I know." Augustus came over to where Rowena stood, her hands twisting nervously by the piano. He placed a comforting arm over her shoulder. Although he found himself a bit foggy on how Rowena's mother was involved in her scheme of using two cats to weed out unsuitable suitors, he knew that Rowena was most certainly *not* evil. "You had a very noble purpose in my mind. A woman shouldn't be married to a man who would lie and cheat to win her. I'll always be honest with you."

"And I with you. But…you must promise me something. You must make a solemn vow."

He squeezed her tighter, trying to stop her trembling. "Anything! Oh, goodness, Rowena, you're trembling. If this courtship is moving too fast—"

"Whatever I show you tonight must never, ever be

told to another living soul. Do you promise?"

"Of course," Augustus replied automatically, although he had no idea what she could show him that would be so dire.

"Well...I—perhaps you'd better sit. Yes, let's get this over with." Rowena seemed to be steeling herself for something unpleasant. "Only my parents have ever seen this."

Augustus nodded, lost for words. He sat where she pointed, a comfortable wingback chair by the warm ashes in the fireplace. He cast an eye over the portrait hanging above the piano as Rowena paced in front of it. Her father and mother looked so in love. And those blue eyes! Rowena was the spitting image of her mother.

He frowned. Those eyes, indeed. He knew he was besotted with Rowena, thinking about every detail of her face and every phrase she uttered, but surely he'd seen someone else recently with eyes that exact shade of blue?

"I know you're already aware of my secret, but seeing the transformation will probably shock you. There's brandy in the kitchen if you need it."

"Transformation? Brandy?" Augustus turned his eyes back to his hostess and swallowed the scream that wanted to rip from his lungs.

His beautiful beloved was withering away! Without warning, without blinking, she was shriveling in her dress until layers of fabric puddled on the floor. "Rowena!" He rose from his chair so fast he knocked it over, sending its legs to the ceiling as his hit the floor. He scrabbled at the folds of her dress and petticoat, aware that something was moving among them. "Oh, God. Oh, God, what..." His prayer was broken and unformed, the same as his thoughts.

"Mew?"

Augustus peeled aside the last skirt in the pool of clothing and discovered Tiger's double. The Tigress, as he'd begun to think of her. "What devilment? What parlor trick?" he spluttered, looking around the room for Rowena.

The cat stared up at him, fur puffed out in fear, blue eyes wide.

Blue eyes.

Augustus' head whirled to the painting above the fireplace and back to the cat.

"R-Rowena?" he stammered through cold lips.

The little beast purred and nodded.

As the room swirled and went dark, Augustus' final thought was that he should go find the brandy in the kitchen. He was going to need it.

****

"Augustus?" Rowena crouched over him, dress pulled clumsily over her head, her underthings still lying on the floor. She patted his cheeks. "I wonder if Isabelle left any smelling salts," she fretted.

"What?" The man was mumbling and slowly stirring, head rocking feebly as he regained consciousness.

"Oh, thank heavens! You fainted."

He stilled.

"I supposed it would be a shock, even if you knew it was coming." Rowena tenderly smoothed back his hair. He was so handsome, even with his eyes closed.

The eyes flew open, and he bolted up fast enough to send her springing back. "I *didn't* know it was coming! Wh-what happened? What sort of sorcery was that?"

Rowena scooted out of his path as he scrambled to

his feet. "It's not sorcery. It's…divine providence, I suppose. But what do you mean, you didn't know it was coming? You said you figured out my secret," she protested, a sick feeling gnawing through her. *What could he mean? He didn't know? Have I just ruined everything? My life? My first and probably last attempt to love someone?*

"I knew you had a second cat! You have Tiger and Tigress, a decoy. One who roams about, attracting the attention of suitors…" Augustus trailed off. "Why did you want to attract their attention? Were you luring them here to…" He floundered.

Her face flamed. "That is an unworthy thought, whatever you're thinking, Mr. Warwick."

He shook himself. "No, no, I suspected that if you had some beastly fellow call on you with a bell round Tiger's neck, you'd show them the other and send them away. It'd be a way to keep them chasing after a cat, not you."

Rowena shook her head, sadness creeping across her face. "No, Mr. Warwick." It felt wrong to call him Augustus now, even though only this morning she'd kissed him in view of the town, in view of lordly Matthew Raine, who would be sure to ruin her reputation after tonight, after the inevitable end. With a hard swallow, she forced the tremble from her voice. "I wanted to observe the men who have been pursuing me for years. A woman is property to her husband, to the wrong kind of husband. I know I'm not normal for believing that a woman should have her own thoughts, her own work, her own property…" Her eyes blurred, and she turned away to blink a tear from them. "I wanted to see how men would treat a 'lesser' being. You treat women as equals, and animals as if they were human. I would feel safe entrusting myself to someone like that."

There was silence in the cozy parlor, with only sounds of night birds outside and the distant ting of the streetcar's last voyage for the evening.

Hope fluttered limply in her heart.

"I would not feel safe entrusted to you." The words dragged from him.

Hope shattered, exploding like a smashed vase. "Why?" She whipped around to face him.

"You are not—you are not fully human! You became a cat. No, no, I can't have seen it. But I did." Augustus paced, wringing his hands, then tugging on his hair, spastic fingers pushing it from his eyes. He turned and faced her, brokenhearted eyes boring into hers. "What did you do? How?"

"My mother saved a cat's life. It seemed to give her one of its own. When I was born, this gift, or this curse, passed to me. I don't know, Mr. Warwick. She didn't know. But I do nothing evil or even mysterious to have this ability."

"Nothing evil? For man, God's highest creation, to slip into the form of a lower being? Oh no, there's darkness somewhere."

"Perhaps. But not from me." Anger and sadness mingled. "Can God not use what was intended for evil for good? Can He not do things beyond man's comprehension? What if there are others out there like me? I doubt they will publicize it. You are living proof of what would happen if we shared this secret, this harmless, innocent secret!" she spat.

"Nonsense."

"Salem."

The name of the accursed trials brought a fresh pallor to his cheeks.

"I would never want to see that happen to you."

Rowena wiped her hand across her eyes and then balled it into a fist. "Good. I suppose I can leave town. Go to England, with my father's people. Driven off or hunted down. That's what happens to 'witches.' "

"I never said you were a witch."

"But you think I'm something evil that you cannot be safe around?"

"I...I cannot think. This doesn't make sense."

"You love whimsical things. Music, moving parts, creating your spun sugar fantasies." Rowena reached for his hand in spite of her better instincts. She knew he wouldn't take it. But after so long alone...

He backed away. "I can understand those things. What you've done, I can't fathom. I think...I think maybe I can only understand whimsy of my own making, fantasy that makes sense in nuts and bolts, or boiling points and counterpoint. I'm meant to be alone."

"Oh, Augustus, please. Please don't say that." Tears spilled.

"I'll take your secret to the grave, Miss Mumford." He bowed suddenly, his own eyes bright.

Then he was gone.

She collapsed on the hearthrug, sobbing. Tiger came running, winding himself against her shoulder, scratching pink tongue trying to soothe her tears.

****

Augustus crashed his bicycle into the redbrick of Warwick's Whimsies before staggering off and dragging the bicycle into the dark shelter of Turnbridge Alley.

She lied to me.

No. She never said she was not some foul, shape-shifting creature, half woman, half cat.

She tricked me.

No. I honestly don't believe it's a parlor trick.

It's a miracle. A tiny, incredulous voice whispered under the bitter heartbreak.

No.

Augustus heaved himself onto the squat wooden stool in the dim workshop, miserably huddled amongst tires and chains. Miracles were acts of the divine, for great purposes. Healing. Saving lives. Spreading love. A resurrection, like the Easter miracle. Rowena's "miracle" was the opposite of all that was holy and joyful. Nothing good could come of skulking about on all fours, pretending to be something you weren't.

"Don't even start in on love." Augustus kicked Mr. Graves' bicycle, in for repairs. His son had run it into the mill pond and dragged it home on its side. Now it toppled and fell with a crash, its wheels and handles pointing in opposite directions. "A confused wreck."

Like me.

Chapter Fourteen

Augustus squinted at the morning sun as it warmed Main Street. Up and down the freshly swept street, shops threw open their shutters and doors. After a moment, he retreated from the front of the building and slid back behind the counter, the door still bolted.

The proprietor of a respectable shop should be clean and tidy in appearance.

He looked like he'd fallen asleep in a greasy tool bag or on a heap of rags, mainly because he had. Augustus glanced at the corner table. Rowena would not be coming to sit there.

He looked over the trays of candy and barrels of nuts. Licorice. Of course. Rowena liked licorice, even in cat form. Tiger, a true animal, did not.

"Augustus?"

Of course. His father would choose this day to pay an early morning call. "Go away." Augustus surprised himself. A less heartbroken, less sleep-deprived being wouldn't have dared speak that way to Colonel Warwick.

To his shock, after a moment, his father obeyed.

"Well. I suppose it is the season for miracles," Augustus huffed under his breath.

"You need to lock the alley door. And put in a light. Clear a path. Honestly, son, you—"

"I was wrong." Augustus let out a groan as his father

poked his way through the repair shop into the candy store.

"Wrong? About what?"

"Everything. Miss Mumford. Love. Women. I'm a failure who makes candy and fixes bicycles. Suspicions confirmed. End of report, *sir*." Augustus gave a mocking salute and slammed his way back to the stove. "I may be a failure, but I still do my job. These blasted jelly beans, worthless little bits of sugar, need to be made."

Colonel Warwick sat, blinking in shock. "Oh, Augustus. What happened?"

The softness in his father's voice undid him. Keeping his face firmly to the pot of sugar he was beginning to boil down, Augustus sniffed in. "N-nothing. She's not the one for me. As much as I might wish it."

Obviously, his father couldn't understand the layers of pain and disbelief under the simple words. "What makes you say that? Everything was going so well. I even heard tell there was an er—embrace—yesterday morning?"

"Matthew Raine spreads gossip like he spends money." Augustus prowled around the counter, looking for oranges to juice.

"Was he wrong?"

No. He remembered the way Rowena kissed. No compunctions. No hesitations. Like she didn't care who might see, like they were the only two in the world. The sigh stung as it left his lungs. "No."

"The Mumfords raised their girl well. Peculiar in their ways, some might say, but well. Your mother and I raised you to be a gentleman."

"I was!"

"Then I know your intentions were honorable, as were hers," the older man continued as if he hadn't been interrupted.

"I think…she would have married me. If I'd asked her to." It was short but so perfect. Why did she have to be this way, be cursed? Maybe *he* was cursed, insane.

"But things…went off course last night?" Colonel Warwick suggested delicately.

"Yes. Yes, horribly off course."

There was silence in the shop as Augustus mutilated oranges, taking his pain out on them, leaving them squeezed-out balls of pulp, like his heart.

"Son, let me tell you about the Battle of Cedar Point. Your great-grandfather—"

"Oh. Father. No." Augustus abandoned the fragrant orange mixture he was about to pour into the tiny oval molds. "Not again."

"Hush, boy. Your great-grandfather, a personal friend of our glorious president and general George Washington—"

Augustus considered plunging his head into the bubbling syrupy mess. He'd be horribly disfigured and in terrible pain, but it would silence his father. As he deliberated, his father paced, waving his walking stick.

"Cedar Point was on the verge of capture. Our first stand had been disastrous. But we didn't give up. We fought."

"You weren't even there."

"Our ancestors fought. They wanted something precious—freedom. You want something precious." The colonel looked uncomfortable, face scrunched as if he'd bitten into a rotten apple. "You understand, Augustus. You mustn't surrender after the first defeat. You've

145

gotten farther with her than any man has. That must mean something."

"She trusted me."

"Trusted? As in she *no longer* trusts you? By Jehoshaphat, what could you have done?"

Augustus started at the glistening row of orange gems he'd just poured. What had he done? Refused to believe the unbelievable, despite seeing it with his own eyes? Accuse her of evil practices, even though he'd only seen kindness, brilliance, and beauty in her?

The image of a woman vanishing and reappearing as a cat caused him to twitch suddenly, jumping inside his clammy skin. "I did nothing. Miss Mumford is the one who did something."

"Something you could not forgive?"

"Father, please. I don't have time to discuss it further. I have to get these jelly beans ready by this Sunday. Mrs. Chambers will set every mother in the church on me if I disappoint the little ones on Easter morn."

"Fine. I'll leave you to your *work*," Warwick said the word with disdain. "But I'll remind you that you come from fighting stock, Augustus. You shouldn't take defeat so easily. Cedar Point wouldn't be here today if my grandfather hadn't rallied his men to drive off the Lobsterbacks."

Augustus rolled his eyes. "Rowena isn't a hill to reclaim or an inlet to secure from the British."

"Blast it, you're missing the point. I've said it since you were a boy, you should have been a soldier, you would have learned a thing or two about perseverance."

His father's disappointment and blame hunched Augustus' shoulders under an invisible weight and loosened his tongue. "This isn't about my perseverance, this is about her. Rowena Mumford is a—" Words stopped. His father wouldn't believe him anyway. "She's not a normal woman." *She's a beautiful, wonderful, loving woman. So loving. Warm. Under that reserve, so funny.* He sniffed hard, eyes tearing. "Not the kind of woman you'd want as a daughter-in-law."

Colonel Warwick limped to the front door, shaking his head. "Fool. It was never about what I'd want in a daughter-in-law. It was about what you'd want in a wife. The good Lord knows, you were never what I wanted in a son. Loved you still." With a twist of the lock and a slam of the door, he was gone.

Augustus set down the pot and wooden spoon he'd been holding, staring after his father. In nearly thirty years, that was the first time the word "love" had ever been mentioned.

"The Lord works in mysterious ways, His wonders to perform. Heavenly Father…What are you doing?" Augustus groaned.

No answer. The Lord didn't speak from the clouds these days. Or perform miracles like turning women into cats. That had to be the work of the devil, even if Rowena laid no claim to it.

Too much confusion existed outside his head, Augustus retreated inside his mind, back to the now familiar task of making thousands of brightly colored sweets.

****

Rowena dropped her pen as someone tapped at the door. Her heart leaped with a surge of hope. It could be Augustus. Maybe two days apart had changed his mind?

Her heart sank. If he were going to change his mind

and accept her secret, he would have done it by now.

"Carrie. Come in."

Carrie strode in, looking radiant with her hair in an elegant sweep and her clothes in a looser, more fashionable cut. While still pale and thin, she no longer looked squeezed and pinched, especially since her features were arranged in a wide smile. "Simon and I are going to take the ferry to Gull Island and have a picnic on Saturday. You should come with us. The Young Seminarians are arranging all the food and the fun. Just bring some old shoes and a few rugs to put out for the luncheon."

"I don't think I will, Carrie, but thank you." Rowena smiled, glad to see her friend and pupil so joyful. "I wouldn't be good company just now."

"Mr. Warwick is invited as well."

"Then I assuredly should not come. He…He and I have ended our acquaintance."

Carrie's smile faded. "What? No! I heard that you and he…That is, I heard there was even a kiss."

"I shall have to move." Rowena laughed without mirth, the bitter tang of tears at the back of her throat. "Everyone will remember that I kissed a man before we were properly engaged."

"I can't believe it. I would never in a million years have imagined kind Mr. Warwick was the type of man to jilt a woman or breach his promise."

"He didn't. It was…it was a matter of personal preference, Carrie. I don't bear him any ill will, and neither should you. Some men cannot handle a woman's secrets, her family history."

"Ahh." Carrie nodded with a knowing look. "Madness?"

Rowena hesitated. Was she mad? If she said she could turn into a cat, but could not, that would be madness, yes. But she could. She wished right now that she could not. She'd prayed for God to take the affliction from her. He had not seen fit to listen. "No, Carrie. Another burden."

Carrie's eyes narrowed. Rowena knew she was imagining all sorts of things. Was there a man in her past? Was she no longer "virtuous"? Was there a secret child or a secret divorce? That was what everyone would think when they discovered Augustus had kissed her in broad daylight and shunned her by night.

She preferred being the witch.

"I'm sorry," Carrie said simply, voice gentle. "I know what it is like to feel lonely, then find friends. To lose one so dear…" Carrie held her arms open.

With a sob, Rowena rushed into them.

****

"Oh. Good morning, Miss Earnshaw." Augustus had opened his shop the next day. One day of lost business he could afford, but two in a row with no proper reason might make people in predictable Cedar Point think he was unreliable.

He hadn't been idle in his seclusion. His apron bore stains of every flavor and hue. His fingertips were burnt and blistered from mucking about with scalding syrup and sugar. Sleep was forgotten, as was eating, bathing, and shaving. As he looked up from his work to greet his first customer of the day, he realized he must look a fright. Miss Earnshaw stood in the doorway as if choosing whether to flee or approach.

"Good morning." She bobbed her head stiffly. Gathering her handbag and shawl to her sides as if girding her loins for battle, she waded in, voice clipped, steps severe. "I spent a good deal of the afternoon with Miss Mumford yesterday."

Tiredness crashed over him like a sudden wave.

"How could you treat her so cruelly, Mr. Warwick? Surely whatever secrets she has in her past cannot truly matter now? I know it is not a disease or madness in her family."

"Did she tell you?"

"No. Nor did she tell me your reasons. She speaks of you with such love, despite her broken heart." Angry tears filled the girl's eyes. "Such a lovely woman, not just beautiful, truly kind and good! How can you do this, Mr. Warwick?"

He didn't know. He honestly didn't know, and he was angry that he had no good answer. He was angry that he was being questioned. Anger added barbs to his tongue that didn't belong. "You'll find yourself in the same boat if Trilby hears you speak like this. He likes his women smart but servile. That's why Rowena wouldn't have him and passed him off to you."

With a gasp, she backed up, her angry tears splashing on either cheek.

"I'm sorry. I—"

"Simon Trilby is a fine man who admires my convictions. It is not right that a person, man or woman, should watch an injustice and keep silent. Should Rowena have confided in Professor Trilby, I am sure *he* would be the one asking you how you can treat a woman so cruelly."

"Do you think I'm idiotic enough to want this, Miss Earnshaw? I *love* her. I love her, and I would not care for her past or her health. I would care about the woman herself."

"Then why—"

"If she did not tell you, I will not." Augustus cut the conversation off, crossing his arms over his broad chest.

"If she told you and not me, she trusts you more. She must think you can help her with whatever it is!"

"Well, I cannot. I do not know how to help her. I wish that I could. Now, if you're in my shop, you must want to make a purchase."

"I wanted to see my friend. I thought that I could claim you as one, Mr. Warwick. It seems Miss Mumford and I were both misled." She turned on her heel and left the shop.

Augustus sank back, leaning against the splattered counter, Carrie's words rattling in his brain and stabbing his heart.

Friends. He'd always been a friendly man, but for the first time, with Rowena, Simon, and yes, even Carrie, he'd felt himself growing beyond simple friendliness. They belonged together, an odd mix of people, suddenly made less odd simply by having others of the same ilk around them.

If she told you and not me, she trusts you more. She must think you can help her with whatever it is. Rowena needing help? His heart throbbed as he thought of Carrie's bitter words. *But how could I help Miss Mumford? I'm no magician. I cannot cure her.*

If you think it needs curing, then it is a disease, and you said health didn't matter, the woman mattered.

This is not a medical ailment, but a mystical one. She claims it was passed from mother to child.

Then again, she can't help it, as she could not help catching a disease. Rowena said she uses her strange ability for good. Which means she controls it, and one doesn't control a disease.

Augustus pushed off the counter and stormed up the backstairs to his flat, fearful of alienating more customers with his unkempt appearance. Maybe a good scrub and a fresh set of clothes would settle his mind. Right now, it was running in a frantic circle, always over the same ground.

I love Rowena. I have every reason to trust her. She was honest about everything, even the most unsavory secret. I believe her when she says her plight is nothing evil.

But such things are impossible. If they exist, they must surely be evil.

Where does that leave me?

****

"Carrie, leave me in my gloominess. It'll fade, I assure you. Broken hearts do." Rowena smiled bravely. "I appreciate that you tried to talk to Mr. Warwick, but his mind is made up."

"But his heart is yours!" Carrie insisted, pulling Rowena to her feet. "Get up from your writing and go to him."

"No, it would be shameful, a woman pursuing a man like that. Trying to convince him…" Rowena trailed off. So much of what he said was excusable, given the shock, given the town they grew up in, the looming pall of Salem that never quite faded. He saw a woman slip from human to cat. She had no scientific explanation. It was an act of the divine or the devil. Perhaps if she told him the whole story? No. No, why risk further pain?

Carrie stood before her, studying her as if she could peer inside her mind. "Rowena, whatever secret you have, you could share with me. I would take it to my grave. If it was a sin, I would pray for you. If it was an affliction, I would bear it with you. But I would not leave. I love you, dearest friend. What is more, today Mr. Warwick told me he loves you. He does not want this secret to have come between you, but he thinks he can do nothing to put it right."

"He's correct. There is nothing any person can do. As for God? Well, I have prayed, Carrie. This burden is mine and shall not be lifted." Rowena shook her head and turned away, trailing slowly back to the piano. She felt happiest there, fingers unable to strike the keys, but close to the source of happy memories, under the gaze of her parents' painted eyes. "If he changes his mind, he will come to me."

Carrie stamped her foot, causing Rowena to look up, startled.

"No! That is…that is damsel-in-distress thinking, Rowena. We are not those helpless maidens. You showed me that. We are women with brains, hearts, and opinions. We are women with voices! By Heaven, one day soon, women shall vote, women shall work, women shall stand in court and in operating theaters! Women shall go to the men they love and tell them to stop being pigheaded fools." Carrie stormed back to the piano, all her past temerity vanishing at the sight of her hero in distress. She pushed Rowena toward the stairs. "Would you fight for your rights, Rowena Mumford?"

"Yes, of course," Rowena blurted.

"Then fight for your love. I don't care if I have to stay here all night, I *will* see you step on the streetcar and make your way back to the arms of Augustus Warwick."

****

Augustus, feeling like a wrung sponge but looking presentable, put on one last batch of sugar, keeping the heat on low. He'd moved through the day in a haze, serving a few customers, bagging his brightly colored jelly beans, and still marching in a mental loop, torn between begging Rowena's forgiveness and trying to force her from his mind.

The door shut softly behind him, perfectly timed to the fizzle and snap of the streetlamp.

Hm. Must've forgotten to lock up at the end of the evening. It was nearly eight now. Augustus glanced at the small clock over the stove.

The customer didn't call out a greeting. For a moment, his heart sped up. "Rowena?" he whispered.

"No. Rowena, is it? Already calling her by her Christian name, though maybe that in itself is a lie. Girl is a heathen, isn't she?"

Augustus whirled. Matthew Raine was sneering at him as he drew the shade over the shop window.

"What do you want, Matthew?"

"Nothing much. A chat about the woman you stole from me."

Augustus held his tongue. He wanted to retort that the woman in question wasn't property to steal, and if she was, she was no longer his.

"Maybe I should thank you. If a girl is so loose with her virtue…But what can you expect, being trotted around to those savage places, India and the like."

Anger fogged his brain. "Miss Mumford is no heathen, nor are the people of India savage. They are different. So is she. Well-traveled and well-educated. Things you cannot appreciate."

"Oh, but the soldier's-son-turned-candymaker is so

much more refined?" Raine finished pulling the third shade, blocking the two display windows and the door's glass with large canvas blinds.

Augustus drew himself up. "Does one need to be refined to recognize a lady? Surely even the poorest beggar can spot a queen when she passes."

Matthew threw his head back. "Look at you, with your fancy talk. Spending time with Trilby and his bookworms? And *lady*? Why, once everyone realizes how she cozied up to you—and for what reason, no one will ever call her a 'lady' again."

"What do you mean?" Augustus was now at arm's length from Raine. His fingers itched to grab the man by the collar and toss him into the street.

"Well, she has the money and the house. She has the beauty. What do you bring to the equation besides your tinker's kit and your barrels of sugar? She needs a certain respectability, is that it?"

"I don't know what you're implying, but you need to leave. Now." Augustus knew exactly what he was implying, and his stomach twisted. "Rowena is a lady, through and through. Get it through your dandified skull. She chose a simple man instead of a rich swine. That says more about *you* than it does her."

The sudden lunging punch knocked Augustus backward, rocking him off balance. His head struck the hard wooden counter as he careened on his heels, and then the world went black.

He didn't see Matthew clutch his bleeding knuckles, look at the rapidly spreading pool of blood surrounding Augustus' still form, and then hurry to the front door. With a twist of the lock, Raine shut the door behind him and slunk off in the dark.

Nor did Augustus see the sugar in the pot start slowly creeping over the rim, sputtering as it hit the flames.

Chapter Fifteen

Rowena walked around the churchyard for the tenth time.

"Wouldn't this give Augustus something to say? Not to mention the rest of the town. There she is, the witch, cavorting with the dead." Rowena stopped to look at her parents' headstone, a simple white cross, turning gray with the first few years of weathering. "All that's missing is the black cat." She chuckled, placing a tender hand on the smooth stone. "Tiger stayed home, Mama, Father. But the cat? The cat is always with me, isn't it? And that's all that I'll ever have."

The bell tower tolled eight thirty. From the hill behind the church, Cedar Point's streets were dark with occasional pinpoints of light on the second stories, the flats above the shops still lit while the bachelors cooked their suppers and cramped couples rocked babies to sleep above family stores. If she turned the other way, looking toward the residential area of the city, half the houses were still lit, but most had drawn the shades.

"Either way, I will have to walk home. The streetcar made its last run." She smiled wanly at the stone before she wrung her hands. Augustus' shop on Main Street couldn't be picked out of the dark squares beneath her gaze. Was he up in his flat? Still cleaning up downstairs? Perhaps playing something in his workshop as he tried to soothe a broken heart.

"If he has a broken heart because of me, and I have one because of him, surely it means that we are the only two who can fix each other? Mama? Father? Oh, send me a sign. Tell me to go home, to go to him, tell me *something.*"

The grave stayed silent, and a chilly wind blew a fragrant breeze around her pale-green dress, almost unsettling the hat she had pinned over the hastily curled bun on the back of her head. With her unusually keen senses, Rowena caught another scent, so faint that she doubted a purely human nose would have caught it. The smell of sweet, sticky burning, like blackened caramel.

"If he tells me to leave, then I shall. I shall leave Cedar Point and go to continue your work," Rowena murmured, placing gloved fingers to her lips and then to the carved letters that spelled out her parents' names. "Perhaps that was the Lord's plan all along. I wasn't meant for a place like this. There's nothing for me to do here but hide away from the rest of the world."

****

In a matter of minutes, Rowena had made her way from the churchyard to the silent shops of Main Street. It would be scandalous for a single woman to be seen calling upon a single man at this hour, even worse than a man calling upon a woman.

Why? Rowena grit her teeth as she thought of the injustices the sexes heaped upon each other. If a man came to serenade a woman, to plead his cause at her window, it would have been a moonlit scene from Shakespeare. Should a woman do the same? She'd be called a lunatic at best and a lewd drunkard at worst.

"I shouldn't have listened to Carrie." Carrie had inched her up the stairs and into one of her better dresses, with a constant reminder that meek and quiet women marry the Matthew Raines of the world and become a piece of household furniture.

Furniture didn't risk arrest. Rowena sucked in a deep breath as she stopped before Warwick's Whimsies.

An acrid tinge of smoke hit the back of her throat. "Augustus?" Worry of one kind was replaced with another. Rowena hurried to the shop door and knocked on it. "Augustus! Mr. Warwick?" The smoky smell was more unpleasant now, getting thicker by the second. There was no answer. *Perhaps he's upstairs*, Rowena thought, stepping back and looking up at the little second-floor flat. No lights. Shutters open.

But the blinds were drawn in the shop. That was unusual. Augustus never covered his two large display windows at night. He flipped the wooden sign on the door to read "Closed" but left the windows uncovered, no doubt hoping to remind customers what sweet delights awaited once he reopened the following day.

Rowena jiggled the door's handle. The door was locked but not bolted, she could tell by how much it moved about in the jamb. Worry that simmered bubbled over. Augustus must be on the premises. Light streamed around the edges of the blinds, giving the place a tawny muted glow. So, the door was locked but not bolted, which meant he hadn't ventured upstairs for the night, a supposition borne out by the open shutters and dark second-story windows.

So why didn't he answer? Was he avoiding her? Dealing with a fire in the kitchen?

"The workshop. He must be round the back." Rowena hitched up her skirts and ran to Turnbridge Alley, searching for the shop's side entrance. Gray smoke seeped under the doorway of the repair shop.

There was a fire inside the building. Bone-deep instinct screamed that Augustus was inside the building, too, and if he wasn't answering, and if the building was silent (as it was) then something was wrong.

Two courses of action popped into Rowena's mind. One, she could start screaming for help and banging on windows and doors, hoping that someone was working late in one of the apparently deserted shops on Main Street.

Or she could get into the building herself and put out the fire.

The next second, her slender shoulder met the heavy wooden door. The second after that, she found herself sitting in a puddle in the alley. "Weak body of a woman!" she hissed, picking herself up and ignoring her soaking wet bottom. "Augustus! Please, can you hear me? Open up!" She twisted the wrought iron knob on the thick wooden door, only to yank her hand away. The metal was hot to the touch.

That does it. Rowena looked up in prayer as she clutched her hand. The flutter of a white gauzy curtain caught her eye. One of Augustus' back windows was open. One flight up.

Cats had no trouble getting into places they should not be. With a frantic glance around the alley, Rowena squeezed herself into the darkest corner of it. Her form rippled, and in seconds, her dress and undergarments lay in a heap, and a black cat streaked along the alley fence, balanced on a window ledge, then another, and with a desperate leap—sailed through the narrow gap in the window.

Rowena stayed in cat form as she zipped through the

bachelor's flat and down the stairs. Blessing her tiny lungs and her ability to stay low to the floor, she made her way under a fog of smoke into the candy shop.

She stopped dead, heart falling and breaking more than it already had.

Augustus lay flat on the floor, a circle of blood around his head. "Mrooow!" a wailing whine ripped from her throat as she ran to him, sniffing his face.

He stirred, coughing.

Even as she ran from him, searching for the source of the fire, she couldn't stop the purr that sang through her chest. He was alive. She had one more chance— if she could save him.

The kitchen in the back of the shop was partially afire, but thank God, the flames seemed to have made their way from a burnt-out pot on the stove through the paper sacks Augustus used for his customers and spread to the workshop area. Rowena knew that in seconds, the fire would ignite the gas from the stove or spread toward the body. Flashing into human form without thought for her state of undress, Rowena turned off the stove and put the sink taps on full. She grabbed an armful of singed and smoking tea towels and aprons, and stuck them in the sink, soaking them to throw over the fire as it smoldered along the floor.

****

Augustus opened his eyes. They stung. He tried to ask what had happened, why he was on the floor. His throat made a horrible rasping grate. He coughed and his head throbbed.

His ears and nose still worked. Smoke. Crackling. Slapping?

He tried to sit up but could only turn his head.

An angel, bathed in misty gray with a halo of bright orange light was fleeing into his workshop, beating her white wings.

She looked just like Rowena.

Rowena.

Though his head was muddled, Augustus had one thought penetrate the haze. *Something is wrong with me. I may be dying. I may be dying, and I'll never see Rowena again.*

Augustus forced himself to his side, only to retch and see a curtain of blackness. He fought through it, pushing himself to his hands and knees, suddenly aware how hot the floor was under his palms.

Fire.

My shop is on fire!

Adrenaline cleared his head, and a swirl of thoughts came cascading back—Raine's cowardly sneak attack, the unexpected punch, the pain in his head. The stove. He'd been finishing up a batch of syrup when Raine arrived.

And the angel who looked like Rowena?

A crash sounded from the back, a tumble of metal mixed with a feminine shriek.

"*Rowena!*"

"Augustus! Stay low, it's almost out."

Lurching forward, staying in a crouch both from necessity and because of her warning, Augustus grabbed the fire bucket from under the counter. He showered sand over the charred bits of counter and floor, then moved to the repair shop.

The dark, smoky room threatened to suffocate him. He couldn't see his savior, only flashes of white. They were not wings, but wet towels and aprons, not to mention bare arms.

"I'll manage. Get out of here!" Augustus yelled, throat raw.

"Not until you do!"

****

Though the amount of smoke was impressive, the actual fire was rapidly coming under control. The smoke was fading. Calm was overcoming desperation.

With a frightened squeak, Rowena realized that she was inside, and her dress was still in the alley. Thankful for the smoke, she took a sooty, soaked apron and slid it over her head.

"I think it's out," Augustus rasped.

"Must get air into the place." Rowena went toward the alley entrance, then paused and put her back to the wall. The apron covered her front—just.

Augustus opened the door and sighed as fresh air hit his face. "How did you know about the fire? How did you get in?"

"I came to town to—to speak to you." Rowena hung her head, hiding behind her hair, now hanging loose after battling the fire and her transformation. "I called and knocked, but you didn't answer. I smelled the smoke. I was worried about you."

"You had every right to be worried. Matthew Raine punched me, right in the jaw. Knocked me for six. I must've struck my head on something." Augustus felt his head with a frown, wincing when his fingertips came away with congealed blood on them. "I'm assuming he left without realizing I still had a pot of sugar on the stove."

"I wondered why I smelled burning caramel," Rowena mumbled.

"But the door was locked? How did you—"

"Cat. The upstairs window." She kept her answers short, fearing his silence, or worse, his rejection.

Neither came. He came, stepping over to her, his hands searching for hers. "You were right. You said it wasn't evil. When I opened my eyes tonight, I saw an angel. A lovely white angel, covered in smoke and flame, like the pillar of cloud leading the Israelites by day and the column of fire by night."

In spite of the earnestness in his voice and the love in his eyes, Rowena had to laugh. "Oh, my dear. How hard were you hit?" She reached for his head, and he bowed it, resting his forehead to hers. Her fingers discovered a long gash under a lump. He grunted in pain when her hand made contact, but he was still smiling.

"Hard enough to have sense knocked into me. I love you. I—I thought I was dying. I couldn't bear the thought of never seeing you again. Never telling you."

"B-but what about my secret?" Rowena demanded, pulling away.

"It saved my life. It saved your mother's life. Without her, you wouldn't be here. And without you…I wouldn't be here. Rowena, I—"

As Augustus pulled her to his chest, she scuttled away, back firmly against the wall.

"Rowena, please. I'm sorry I doubted you."

"It's not that. It's that…My dress. Is in the alley."

"Hm?" Augustus frowned, puzzled.

"My dress. It's in the alley. I'm in here." Rowena bit her lip. Her swain was still staring at her with confused eyes. "My dress is in the alley, and I'm not in it. I'm in one of your aprons, Augustus, and nothing else!"

Comprehension dawned. He hastily backed up, eyes

wide. "I'll go fetch it, shall I?"

"That would be most kind, Mr. Warwick."

He paused as he left the smoky room, eyes twinkling. "After all of this, I think we should stick with Christian names, don't you?"

"I suppose." She had to laugh.

"Although...Mrs. Rowena Warwick has a certain musical quality to it, don't you think?"

Heart fluttering, Rowena had to admit that she did.

Chapter Sixteen

The end of the week was frantic. The shop owners on Main Street pitched in with quiet, determined Cedar Point steadfastness, working until Warwick's Whimsies was as neat as a pin. Matthew Raine had suddenly had a burst of industriousness and claimed he couldn't be spared from the mill.

"He'll have to show his face on Easter Sunday," Augustus said, counting pink, green, and yellow jelly beans into a bag.

Rowena tied it off with a ribbon. "You should tell the police."

"I might. I might not." He grinned at her over their table, still in the sunny shop corner.

Rowena smirked in return. "Devilish."

He passed an almost empty spool of ribbon to Tiger, who chased it across the shop floor. "Aren't I? I don't think you mind if there's a touch of the incorrigible about me."

"Do you mind that there is a streak of the impossible around me?" Rowena giggled.

"Not in the slightest." Augustus rose enough to reach her lips across the candy-strewn table. She tasted of licorice. All of the black jelly beans went directly in Rowena's pile.

"Augustus. M'dear." Colonel Warwick announced his arrival. "How many troops are ready for battle?" He

166

pointed to the pretty pink bags with their white and green ribbon.

"One hundred and fifty, give or take," Rowena replied, extending her hand to her future father-in-law. Her hand sparkled with a small, square-cut garnet ring set in a heavily filigreed band.

"Ahh. It looks lovely on you. That'll catch the light when you teach those little ones to play. Augustus tells me you want to keep giving lessons.'

"I do. It has nothing to do with how well your son can keep me, Colonel. I would get up to mischief if I wasn't gainfully occupied." Rowena dipped her head to hide her smile.

"Hmm." The gruff old soldier's tone made it obvious he doubted that. "You're one of those newfangled women under that pretty smile, m'dear. Want to work. Want to vote. Well. Perhaps that'll suit my boy. He has a love of newfangled things."

"I certainly have a love of this one." Augustus wrapped his arm around his betrothed's shoulder.

"Now, now. Save that for after Sunday when the good reverend announces it. The tongues in this town wag enough as it is."

Augustus sighed. "Father, did you come here with some purpose in mind?"

"Your mother sent me round to ask if you want pea soup or tomato for the first course."

"Well, I'm partial to Mother's split—"

"Not you." The colonel glared Augustus to silence. "Rowena?"

"Pea soup sounds wonderful."

****

Easter Sunday burst forth like a morning glory at

sunrise.

Rowena rubbed the sleep from her eyes as Tiger tugged open the sash that held her heavy brocade drapes closed. Although she'd gotten home at midnight last night (after ensuring that every jelly bean was prettily wrapped and ready to distribute), Rowena felt energized.

After years of loneliness and whispers, months of unwanted suitors, and weeks of nerve-wracking pursuits, the minister would read out the banns this Sunday morning, announcing her forthcoming marriage to Augustus Warwick.

She slid on her Easter ensemble, a white dress with tiny pink roses, topped with a small pink hat with swaths of white tulle. "Very bridal," she murmured to her reflection. "It's just missing one thing."

Rowena tripped lightly down the stairs and into the parlor, making for the ornamental box on the mantel. She lifted out the beautiful silver bell on its glimmering chain. Brimming eyes turned toward the painting of her parents. "Father got this for you in China, didn't he, Mama? Outside a little temple." Her mother often wore it. She said it reminded her of their early marriage, of traveling together, helping people.

Rowena gasped in dismay as she went to fasten the necklace. The tiny clasp wouldn't hold. "Oh...Oh!" Her sad cry turned to laughter. Augustus would fix it in seconds. He always had tools with him in his bicycle cart, and he'd use it to deliver the hundreds of bags of jelly beans to the church.

As she tucked the necklace into her white purse, Rowena mused that Augustus would repair her necklace and place it around her neck.

"A bell round my neck and a ring on my finger. He has belled the tiger…well, the tigress."

Epilogue

"Thank you. Thank you. Yes, indeed, it happened rather quickly. A spring wedding? June, perhaps." Augustus hadn't talked to so many people in years nor answered so many questions. The delight of Easter and Easter baskets seemed to be the second-most popular topic of conversation that Sunday morning.

The leading topic was the sudden (but not wholly unexpected) engagement announcement.

"Of all the men she could have, why him?"

"He is rather handsome. If someone would do something about his hair."

"He'll be well-placed now, with her money."

Augustus sighed. He was glad all of the comments he heard weren't directly addressed to him or his beautiful bride-to-be. The vast majority were well-wishers. Augustus wondered if one could sprain one's wrist from shaking so many hands so heartily. At this point, all of the iron grips were blurring together.

"Congratulations."

"Th—" Augustus stopped. This handshake wasn't right. It wasn't hard. It was—papery. He looked up, into the wincing eyes of Matthew Raine. He looked down, to find his fist stuffed full of notes.

"What a glorious day to announce a wedding, old man. Ha, and who'd have thought it would be you before Ruger, Trilby, or I? Wonderful. Must be going."

Augustus dug his fingers into Matthew's palm, crinkling the money. "You and I have a few things to discuss."

"My father is right there." Matthew jerked his head back to the open doors of the church.

"So is my father. So is Sergeant Dawkins." Augustus wrung Matthew's hand as if he hoped to pop the bones from their skin. "This isn't about our parents."

"Of course, I was selfishly unhappy at first, but now I'm delighted for my old school chum," Matthew said loudly, voice hale and hearty, causing heads to turn.

"We were never that friendly. We're certainly not friendly now. You nearly burnt my shop to the ground."

"I didn't know I'd started a fire. How could I have? I punched you, Auggie. I'm sorry."

"You didn't stay to see that I was all right. Don't call me Auggie. We're not friends. You're not forgiven. Not yet."

Matthew laughed nervously. "Let me aid you on your way—" He dropped his voice. "—to forgiveness, Warwick, please." Voice back to normal volume, he added, "Let me offer you a wedding present early, dear friend!"

"You can't buy me off. You almost burnt my shop to ashes and could have killed me if I hadn't woken up in time."

"That will pay for a trip to Europe. Wouldn't you like to take your bride to Paris?"

"She's been."

"Name your price. Any price."

"I'll ask Rowena, but my guess is that she'll know already. She has amazing hearing."

Rowena chose that moment to take Augustus'

elbow, a smile on her face that didn't reach her eyes. "How kind of you to offer your congratulations, Mr. Raine." She kept Augustus' elbow tucked through her own as she leaned forward, ostensibly to offer her hand to Matthew. As he bowed over it, she hissed, "The money goes to an orphanage in Pondicherry, India, and a scholarship for the Cedar Point School, split evenly between a boy scholar and girl scholar, to send them to college. Renewed annually. And take the credit for it, Mr. Raine. I'd like it to be in your name. People will see that you are forward-thinking, that you treat women as individuals, not objects to be…fought over. Make sure it is set up by the end of the week, or I'll consult with my correspondents in Cincinnati. R. Mumford, Esq., is much respected in legal circles."

Augustus chuckled at the cold gleam in her eyes and the beautiful smile on her face. Raine flinched.

"I'll see to it on Monday morning. Tomorrow. In fact, I'll handle the school matters; you take this money to send to that orphanage. That should settle this little misunderstanding."

"Indeed." Augustus crushed his rival's fingers once more, this time pulling back with the money in his palm. "But purchase your candy elsewhere. Just to be safe."

Matthew looked at Rowena for a long moment before returning his gaze to Augustus' hard face. "Better you than me, Warwick." He bowed low to Rowena, then trotted away, back to the safety of his parents and their air of wealth and respectability.

"Do you think so?" Augustus took both of Rowena's hands in his own, picturing her in a different white dress but in that same location, standing in front of the church.

"Better that I wed you than Mr. Raine?" Rowena

shook her head, seemingly unable to voice how horrific that would be. Instead, she threw herself into his arms, locked her arms across his shoulders, and kissed him.

"Rowena Mumford! What will people say?" Augustus chided with a twinkle in his eye.

Rowena winked as she flicked the bell around her neck. "That you won, my love. That we both did."

A word about the author…

Bestselling author M. Culler can't stick to just one genre. She writes fantasy, mystery, and all flavors of romance. M. Culler lives in historic Chester County, Pennsylvania, where potentially haunted battlegrounds and 17th-century buildings serve as never-ending inspiration. M. Culler lives for her two brilliant children (mini-bookworms), her gorgeous husband (who must hold the world's record for patience), her endlessly entertaining students, and her wonderful friends and family. If she's not hunched over a laptop, you'll find her baking up a storm in the kitchen, playing board games, or watching Brit Coms. Soli Deo Gloria.

mcullerauthor@gmail.com
Newsletter:
https://ghostsintheink.wixsite.com/mculler
Facebook:
https://www.facebook.com/MCullerGhostsintheink
Amazon:
https://www.amazon.com/M.-Culler/e/B07MZ7KP6S
Goodreads:
https://www.goodreads.com/author/show/18749746.M_Culler
Bookbub:
https://www.bookbub.com/profile/m-culler
Twitter:
https://twitter.com/MCullerauthor
Instagram:
https://www.instagram.com/mcullerauthor/
Reader's Group:
https://www.facebook.com/groups/3369871793294694

Thank you for purchasing
this publication of The Wild Rose Press, Inc.

For questions or more information
contact us at
info@thewildrosepress.com.

The Wild Rose Press, Inc.
www.thewildrosepress.com